ABOUT THE AUTHOR

Valerie G Miller lives in Brisbane, Australia, with her husband and daughter, after relocating from Sydney. In 2021, she completed a Master of Letters in Creative Writing at Central Queensland University, Australia.

She writes contemporary women's and romance fiction, as well as magical realism novellas and short stories.

Her dog Mischa and cats, Daisy and Miss Lily, are her writing companions. You will always find a novel and a notebook filled with ideas and observations tucked away in her handbag. She believes that stories are medicine for the soul and kissing books make the world a happier place.

Visit her at www.valeriegmiller.com

facebook.com/valeriegmillerwriter

twitter.com/valeriegmiller

instagram.com/2bwriting

ALSO BY VALERIE G MILLER

Sweet Treats Chocolate 2021 Short Stories

EVERYTHING IN BETWEEN

STORIES OF FAMILY, LOSS AND LOVE

VALERIE G MILLER

Blushing Daisy
BOOKS

Cover Design from Damonza.com

ISBN: 978-0-6453046-0-2 (Print)

ISBN: 978-0-6453046-1-9 (E-Book)

Seodin, this book is dedicated to you.
Your authentic and honest feedback as the first reader of
these stories helped to make them shine.
You are my truest and dearest fan

VGM

DEAR READER

I've been telling stories since I was little, even before I could read. I would look at the pictures and make up a story. Once I learned to read, there was no stopping me. The more I read, the more of my own stories formed inside my mind. When my family and I moved away from Sydney, the only city we had ever lived in, to Brisbane in Queensland, the need to get my stories out into the world switched on. No longer was I satisfied with writing stories and then filing them away in the bottom drawer of my desk. My goal was to share my work with others. I learned about the craft of writing, enrolled into and completed a Master of Letters in Creative Writing, and started writing short stories.

These short stories are the first wave of my journey to becoming a published author. Mark Twain said, 'Write what you know.' This has and continues to be a starting point for me as a writer. I'm inspired by architecture, images, what I read and watch, and snippets of words I hear out in the field. Although the characters in these stories, along with their emotions, thoughts, relationships, and experiences, are completely fictional, they have been inspired by the world around me. The writer will always leave a piece of themselves in the stories they write. It is part of being an artist.

I'm from an Italian family—my parents emigrated from Europe when Australia sent out a call for immigrants to help populate the nation, after losing devastating numbers of men and women after World War Two. It took a long time to embrace my Italian heritage. As you get older, you become more nostalgic about your past, your memories, and your culture. Bernard Shaw said, 'Youth, is the most beautiful thing in this world—and what a pity it is wasted on children.' I did not see the beauty of my Italian heritage when I was younger. I do now and I'm proud of it, particularly the language. I have sprinkled in Italian words and phrases to ground some of my characters. Where I can, I have conveyed the meaning through the character's action and dialogue. To help you further, I have also included a glossary of terms in the back of this book. As I'm also Australian, and I hope an international reader will enjoy these stories, I have added explanations of specific Australian terms.

These are stories about families, loss, and love. All the themes that make us rich in our own lives. Life is not always perfect, nor are all our experiences and relationships. We are shaped by our families. It's where we learn how to connect with others. To discover all spectrums of emotions. Our lives are a balance of loss and love. The two twist and turn to force us to question, understand, empathise, and connect with each other and to ourselves. The one thing these stories offer is hope. It is hope that helps us to move forward through the stories of our own lives.

CONTENTS

THE STORIES

TRAVELLING WITH OMENS

Elisabetta sat on the roadside, watching Richard pace. His eyes scanned the ground, searching for the car keys. He stopped and ran his hands through his corkscrew, sun-bleached hair—a remnant of the summer they'd left behind when they flew to France.

'I cannot believe you did that, Beth!' he yelled at her.

Taking a deep breath, she glanced at the sunset seeping through the cloudy sky. She got up and opened the boot of their second-hand Citroën—now stalled at a crude angle next to a vast field of lucerne—and pulled out her backpack. The white car covered in Australian flag stickers announced that they were Aussies.

Richard didn't look up, but continued searching frantically for the car keys.

Numerology and omens had always guided Elisabetta. She'd been born into a superstitious Italian family. Her nonna flung holy water around as if it was a life-changing elixir, and would often chant devotions in her dialect as she did so.

Everything about this trip had signposted rejuvenation

and renewal. She'd entered the writing competition on the winter solstice the year before. It had been a rainy Saturday morning and she'd been alone in the apartment she shared with Jade, who had diabetes and smoked copious amounts of pot. Jade's wealthy parents owned the flat, so the rent was cheap.

Elisabetta had met Jade when she started work at Nine Hipsters Jazz Club in Sydney, where they waitressed. She liked the name, and the number nine lived up to its meaning of new beginnings as she and Jade became good friends. Elisabetta loved how Jade didn't take life seriously. Plus, she laughed a lot.

It wasn't until Jade brought Elisabetta to her parents' home that life took a turn, and not in a good way.

Wandering around Jade's family's mansion at Point Piper, she realised why Jade didn't take life too seriously. She was rich. Very rich.

After lunch, Jade's mum had cornered her and made her an offer she couldn't refuse: cheap rent in exchange for keeping an eye on Jade, who wanted an apartment of her own. At first, the arrangement solved all Elisabetta's financial problems. She soon discovered it came at a price.

Having been estranged from her own family since she was nineteen, all Elisabetta wanted was a decent, secure home. Throughout her teenage years she had rebelled against the strict expectations and rules set down by her parents. She snuck out to meet friends her parents disapproved of, breaking ridiculous curfews and enduring harsh punishment on her return. Any contact with an Australian boy was vehemently disallowed.

'You will marry a nice *Italian* boy, Elisabetta. One your father will approve of.' Her mother recited this on a regular basis, hoping Elisabetta would learn this expectation by rote. She never did. She dated boys behind her parents' back. A 'nice Italian boy' was code for a repressed life. A continuation of the one she lived under her father's roof. Elisabetta yearned for more. To be independent and creative. To experience the world *her* way, and to discover true, passionate love. To be free from rules.

'*Sta attento a cosa desideria*—be careful what you wish for,' her older cousin, Irena, warned her when she complained about her parents.

Elisabetta's freedom did come. But at a cost.

One afternoon, her parents returned home early after visiting a sick aunt in Canberra. They walked in on Elisabetta kissing her new boyfriend, Ethan, on her unmade bed. Elisabetta's life shattered like the vase she threw at her father when he picked up Ethan and slammed him against the wall.

Releasing Ethan, he stormed towards her and slapped her. Over the years her father would shout while setting down harsh punishments, but he never hit her. She begged her mother for support. There was nothing. Instead, her mother avoided all eye contact.

'I hate you.' She pushed her father away. She bellowed at her mother. 'And you're pathetic.' She pulled out a large tote bag and started throwing items into it. 'I'm leaving.'

'If you leave this house, you will never be allowed to come back,' her father fumed at her.

'Fine by me. That's exactly what I plan to do.'

Her mother said nothing.

She'd spent the last three years house-sitting, moving from place to place. An urban nomad.

The apartment she shared with Jade in North Sydney overlooked the harbour. The sought-after view was too good to be true. But keeping an eye on a roommate who had

Type 1 diabetes and was a hard-core party girl was stressful. Fear constricted Elisabetta's chest every time she put the key in the lock. She always wondered if this was the day she'd open the door to find Jade unconscious in a pool of her own vomit.

A few months into her glorified babysitting gig, she found herself alone for an entire weekend, unburdened of Jade's antics. Her roommate was on the Gold Coast for a relative's wedding. Elisabetta felt at ease for the first time in months. She went out to get a latte and a muffin and settled in on the enclosed veranda for a weekend of precious peace. The iconic Harbour Bridge loomed ahead—the best company. She'd discovered the writing competition while reading one of Jade's fashion magazines.

What had caught her eye was the fact that the competition was being sponsored by the perfume that her boyfriend, Richard, had bought for her last birthday. Another omen. The winner received the trip of a lifetime: first-class flights to Paris and Venice, including travel on the Orient Express—one of Elisabetta's long-time dreams.

'Why not,' she'd said to Monty, her next-door neighbour's cat, who loved to lie on the wide rendered brick ledge. His long silver legs dangling over the edge. Flicking his tail without a care in the world. Sometimes he wanted attention, other times he ignored you.

Like all men. She thought and sipped her wine.

Monty turned his head and locked his sapphire blue eyes onto Elisabetta. He oozed a feline air of mystery and was often unpredictable. The quintessential omens cats carried. Sometimes he wanted attention, other times he ignored you. He knew how to live without a care in the world. Nothing ever phased Monty. She needed to do the same. To change her life and not be so boring.

The omens were stacking up.

She should have paid more attention to the universe.

THINGS WITH RICHARD hadn't been going well. In her heart, Elisabetta knew he wasn't the right man for her, but loneliness had corrupted her sensibilities. After all, she had no contact with her family, and no time to make friends. She spent every waking hour looking out for Jade and working three jobs, saving all she could for university to get the creative writing degree she yearned for. Richard's interest eased some of the loneliness. But she suspected he knew as well as she did that they weren't right for each other.

They'd met at the jazz club. Richard came in each Wednesday night with his workmates to play music trivia and would always sit at the same table in her section. He flirted with her, and she flirted back. (Mainly to increase her tips.)

One Wednesday night, she'd been stood up for a date and found herself back at the bar on her night off, nursing a drink and chatting with the head barman, Tommy, who was more than happy to lend a sympathetic ear.

Richard walked up to order some drinks. 'Don't you work here?'

'Not tonight,' Elisabetta replied, toasting her glass to nobody in particular. 'Tonight, I decided to spend a wonderful night being stood up.' She took a mouthful of her riesling.

'I can't imagine anyone standing you up.'

Elisabetta smiled. 'Thanks. I needed to hear that.'

Over the next few weeks, they bantered with each other

while she served them at trivia. It didn't take long for Richard to ask her out. He didn't rock her world, but he seemed pleasant enough. He was kind and funny—though this meant he didn't always take life seriously, which irked her a little. After the turmoil of the past few years, this was a man who offered her emotional security, predictability, someone to count on. It suited her.

At first, Richard had been attentive. He never complained about her shift patterns or how they always seemed to be on a different sleep schedule. On her birthday, he stayed up until she got home from the bar at 3 a.m., and was waiting to surprise her with a birthday cake and a bottle of perfume. When she found the writing competition in the magazine a few weeks later, he had poured a glass of wine and toasted to her new life as an author.

But a couple of months after they'd started to introduce themselves as a couple, Richard stopped wanting to do any of the things Elisabetta liked. She hated watching him play footy, but she went every Saturday. If she asked him to do something that she enjoyed, like going to a new exhibition at the state art gallery, he would scoff or whinge about it so much, she'd end up not going herself. At one point, he even started putting her down in front of his mates.

It was around this time that she learned the inconceivable news: she'd won the writing competition.

The revelation had filled her with joy and dread in equal measure. Two tickets. And no one she wanted to take. She doubted Richard would go with her. Her win confirmed the reality: she was truly alone.

The organisers had explained that she needed to take the trip within the next six months. Elisabetta decided to fly out on the last day possible to avoid landing on April Fool's Day. Then her luck turned. The airline cancelled the original flight and rebooked her on a new flight landing in Europe on April 1ˢᵗ. Another omen, of course.

When she told Richard about the win, there was no glass of wine, no celebration. Elisabetta marked the date of their departure on the calendar, ignoring the twist of Richard's mouth and the accompanying lurch in her stomach. The next day, they were leaving the house to attend her friend's engagement luncheon, when Richard suddenly decided that he didn't feel like going. Elisabetta stared at him, but was not shocked. She went alone to the party while he'd gone to the races with his mates. When she discovered he'd lost an obscene amount of money, she'd had enough. After some hurtful things were flung at each other, Richard called it quits and stormed out. Deep down—though her pride was bruised—Elisabetta was relieved.

On New Year's Eve, the pain of the breakup still raw, she watched the midnight fireworks from the balcony and drank with Monty as company.

The buzzer jolted her, but not as much as the voice that came through the speaker when she answered.

'It's me. Can I come up?'

Her finger hovered over the button. What did Richard want? There had been no contact for three months.

'Please?'

She sighed and pressed the button. Having some company wasn't a bad thing. Especially tonight. Besides, she was curious as to why he'd turn up, tonight of all nights.

Richard bounded in. Giddy and excited. He stunk of beer and cigarettes. Grabbing her hands, he fast-talked how he'd made a mistake. That he missed her. He'd sell his souped-up ute and travel with her.

'We could even stay for longer,' he said, grabbing her hands. 'Explore all of Europe. Pick up work where we can.

Let's be adventurous and see the world.' Richard kissed her knuckles with a grin. 'Let's take our lives by the horns.'

'You're drunk and delusional,' she said, trying to process what he was saying. She pulled away and stepped out on the veranda, sucking in the steamy night air.

Maybe it was the entire bottle of riesling she'd polished off. Maybe the laughter and cheers of people down below on the street, happy that a new year had begun. Maybe because it had been three years with no contact from her family. But Elisabetta felt incredibly lonely. This loneliness only added to her anxiety knowing that, in three months, she'd be travelling overseas alone.

'Come on, Beth, what've you got to lose? A family that won't speak to you, babysitter to a pothead, and three dead-end jobs?'

His words stung, but it was as if he'd read her mind.

'What about uni?' she asked weakly, her lack of courage grabbing hold of the excuses.

'Come on. You can write a travel book. You're an excellent writer. You won the holiday—that proves it!' Richard looked so sincere, the conviction in his eyes made her want to cry. She hadn't had anyone believe in her in a long time.

'Look, you said it yourself,' he continued. 'You need to submit a writing portfolio to get into the program at Sydney University. This is your chance to give them something spectacular. A memoir, short stories, poems. Why not?'

'But what about us?'

Richard stepped towards her, took the glass of wine out of her hands, and kissed her. 'We can work it out, I promise. Europe will fix us. It'll just be the two of us.'

It was the beginning of a fresh new year. Look at what the number one, the first of the first, promised: independence, individuality, and initiation. Richard was right. The trip would allow her to pursue her writing career; she could finally become independent, get a place of her own. As long as it paid off. Once she left for the trip, the deal with Jade's mum was off. She would be walking away from a place to live and a job at the jazz club. Elisabetta shook away those thoughts. She had to stop focusing on the negative. Excitement began to bubble up inside her. Travelling around Europe would give her heaps of material to write her travel memoir. She needed to embrace her courage and take charge. This trip would change her life. She could feel it.

She stepped up to Richard and kissed him.

'Okay.'

THE FIRST WEEK delivered all it had promised. Elisabetta revelled in the range of competition events that had been organised: fashion shows, a private viewing at the Musée d'Orsay, an evening at the Moulin Rouge. The five-star hotel in Paris and then the Grand Cipriani Hotel, which overlooked the cool blue waters of the lagoon stretching into the city of Venice, were breathtaking.

Their suite at the Grand Cipriani held uninterrupted views of the central dome of St Mark's Basilica with its bell-tower behind. Elisabetta's excitement made her giddy with anticipation as Richard started spouting off all the things to see while they were here.

He flung himself onto the king-size bed, covered in ivory linen, and laughed at the revelation they could hear the energy and bustle of Piazza San Marco filter in through their window. A sheer curtain fell from the ceiling, framing the large gilded-edged bedhead. The room, with its large crystal chandelier and baroque furniture, oozed decadence.

Elisabetta covered her mouth to muffle her squeals of delight.

The final leg of their journey was the trip on the Orient Express from Venice back to Paris. Elisabetta had ignored the stark warning from the competition's tagline: A Trip of Luxury and Decadence.

But it was as she feared: Richard was a fish out of water.

A month before the trip, Elisabetta had discussed the details with the marketing assistant from the perfume company. As soon as the woman told her to pack suits, ties, and evening dresses, Elisabetta had known Richard wouldn't fit in. He was a tradie whose life was all about rugby league, surfing, and going to the pub. The most luxurious things Richard had ever done were buy Elisabetta a glass of pinot gris at his local and step into a department store in the city to buy the fragrance featured in the competition. And the only closed-in shoes he owned other than his work boots were his black Vans.

From the beginning, the locals in France had looked down on Richard while showering the clever Australian girl who'd written a short story for their top-selling perfume with attention. They made a big noise about a series of advertisements, both in print and for TV, with her story as the inspiration.

What Elisabetta hadn't anticipated was signing over the rights to her story—a requirement in the fine print of the competition's guidelines. She hadn't considered the consequences. Why would she? Not in her wildest dreams had she ever imagined she'd win.

'I was hoping to use the story as part of my portfolio for when I apply to university,' she'd said to Simone, an expat from Paris and the company's public relations manager.

Simone shifted and leaned forward in her expensive

cream Chanel suit. 'I'm afraid we cannot allow this. But ...' She reached into her Prada purse and pulled out her business card. 'Tell the university they can contact me to verify your little story won you this wonderful trip. *Oui?*'

Elisabetta nodded, but her stomach sunk. Yet another omen.

By the time she and Richard had boarded the *Orient Express*, cracks had appeared in their relationship. Elisabetta was doing her best to ignore them. She was enjoying the company of a an older lady, June, who was from Bath and loved reading Jane Austen. As they talked, Elisabetta snuck glances at Richard, who was slumped into the large velvet wing chair, sipping a beer and shredding a napkin. The crushed paper rained onto the fine-weaved carpet.

'You're making a bit of a mess.' June nodded at the pool of paper.

'I'm going back to the cabin.' Richard stood. 'Coming?' He held out his hand.

Elisabetta wasn't in the mood to hear him moan about how boring the train trip was or complain about June.

'You go. I'll be there soon.'

Richard glared at her. 'Whatever.'

Elisabetta swallowed, wrestling with both relief and fear. June offered what she craved—a chance to discuss literature. She'd deal with Richard later.

One hour later, she returned to the cabin. Richard had developed a severe case of the sulks. 'You seem to be having a ball of a time,' he spat.

'Aren't you?'

'They're all snobs.'

'Shh! People will hear you.'

'Who effen cares?!'

Elisabetta sat next to him on the bunk a porter had

made up while they were at dinner. She needed to appease him. She didn't want everyone hearing Richard's outbursts. It embarrassed her.

'I do. I care.' Her words came out sounding anxious.

Richard pulled out his phone and checked his messages. She swallowed down the annoyance starting to seep into her veins. This was supposed to be a memorable trip, but Richard's continued criticisms and sulkiness frustrated her.

'Look, we arrive in Paris tomorrow and then this part of the trip is done. We'll pick up the car and start the *real* trip. Okay?'

'I dunno. Maybe this was a bad idea. I'm thinking about going home.'

Panic punched her in the chest. Go home? Go home to what? A dead-end job. Babysitting a drug addict. 'You said this trip was a chance for me to write and build my portfolio.' She clenched her jaw and took in a long deep breath. The frustration threatened to release the tears she fought hard to contain.

'Well, I haven't seen you write anything.'

'That's not fair. You know I've been busy with all the competition stuff.'

How was this happening? Why did everything good in her life go to shit? Everything had been planned. She'd build up a portfolio while they travelled, apply for university, and then they'd head home in the new year so she could start her degree.

If Richard left, so would his money. They'd planned to use the money from the sale of his ute to help fund the trip. If she used her savings, she'd have nothing left for her uni accommodations and other living expenses. His selfishness stung her. It was his money, but they'd made a deal.

'You promised,' she said.

He looked at her coldly. 'What?'

'You stood in my apartment and promised me we'd do this.'

'Well, I changed my mind, didn't I?'

She could see the hurt in his eyes. Her growing irritation softened a little. He hadn't done anything on purpose. It wasn't his fault he didn't fit in. Her enthusiasm blinkered Richard's needs. She thought about how much she'd loved speaking Italian in Venice, being able to use the dormant language of her parents. Unable to join most of the conversations, Richard had left events early or plodded behind her like a bored personal assistant.

'I'm sorry,' she said. 'I should've been more attentive to you.'

He stared out the window at the shadowy shapes flicking past. Tension built in the silence. Elisabetta studied his back. His broad shoulders were slumped.

'Richard?'

He ignored her.

Tears stung her eyes. Let him go home. Loads of women travelled around Europe alone. Who cares if she had to dip into her savings? She could defer uni for a semester and make up the money then. She was sick and tired of pandering to someone else and giving them control of her. She opened the cabin door and stepped into the hushed hallway. The train rocked under her, stirring a truth she'd buried. She didn't love Richard. She never had. As much as she wanted to be independent and free, she realised that solitude would have to play a part in her journey. She finally understood that her fear of loneliness had shackled her as much as her parents' rules and Richard's incompatibility.

She found herself back in the now-deserted lounge

carriage. She settled in the far corner and pulled her coat tight around her.

IT BECAME official while they were driving down the E421 through Luxembourg to Prüm, their next stop. The competition trip was over and they were three days into their holiday.

Elisabetta swerved the car off the road and slammed on the brakes. She left the engine idling. 'What did you just say?'

Richard turned to her. 'I'm not continuing on the trip,' he said calmly, avoiding her eyes. 'Not with you.'

'With who, then?'

He stared out the windscreen.

'Richard?' Her mind scrambled to make a connection. Find a face. A name.

'Katrina.'

'Your ex-girlfriend?!' Sharp pinpricks stabbed at her skin, and she folded her arms tight against her chest. 'The one who left you for your best mate?' Richard didn't need to answer. His face said it all. 'How? When?'

'I rang her before we boarded the *Orient Express*.'

Elisabetta felt the oxygen leak out of her chest. She steadied her breath. 'You called her *before* we got on the train?'

'This trip was a mistake. I mean coming with—' He stopped.

'Coming with me? Is that what you were going to say?' Anger replaced the hurt flowing through her veins. 'Just be a man and tell me the truth.'

'You want the truth?'

'Yes. All of it.'

'I never stopped loving her.' He reached over and touched the top of Elisabetta's hand, which was gripping the steering wheel. She yanked it away.

'Beth. She missed me too and ...' He took a deep breath. 'She's agreed to travel with me. She's meeting me in Cologne.'

Something primal possessed Elisabetta. At first, she didn't realise that the scream she'd heard had exploded out of her. She yanked the keys out of the ignition and flung herself out of the car. She screamed again, this time at the green lucerne flapping in the wind. Then she propelled the keys into the open field.

SEVERAL HOURS HAD PASSED by the time Elisabetta made her decision, sitting on the side of the E421, smack bang in the middle of Luxembourg.

The options were clear, out in the fresh air. She had two choices: stay chained to her fear, fed by loneliness, or face it and grow in courage. She opened her backpack and pulled out the travel journal she'd bought at the airport before her flight. Inside, the final omen. A quote on the first page:

> *Two roads diverged in a wood, and I—*
> *I took the one less traveled by,*
> *And that has made all the difference.*

Putting on the backpack, she walked down the road alone.

CONNIE FRANCIS SINGS FOR ME

The train pulled in. Still seated, Sofia rubbed the locket. The gold chain rubbed against the back of her neck. She waited for the other passengers to leave, needing the extra time to prepare.

There was a knot of resentment in her chest that was causing her heart rate to rise and tension to smoulder behind her temples.

She didn't have to do this.

She could stay on the train and go back to Sydney. So what if she changed her mind? No one knew she was coming. How could they? Her family didn't even know where she'd been these past ten years.

The train attendant loomed over her. 'Excuse me, we need to clean the carriage for the return journey.'

'Of course.' Sofia snapped the elastic band off her wrist and pulled her thick hair into a messy ponytail. She stood and reached for her bag in the baggage rack above.

Just get off the train, she thought. She inhaled and forced herself forward. *One step at a time. Don't think, just walk.*

The humidity gripped her as she stepped onto the platform. A magpie's warbled song punctured the scent of orange jasmine. The train's wheels ground and shrieked behind her as it inched away from the platform. The heaviness in the air pressed down on her, making her heart race. Sofia steadied her breathing.

There was no turning back. She gripped her bag tightly and tried to ignore the guilt ballooning in her chest. After all, what kind of daughter wouldn't turn up to their own mother's funeral?

WHAT FABRIZIA ANTONELLI lacked in maternal instinct she'd channelled into her business ventures. She'd created a powerful construction empire, and her power had grown with each new urban development. Fabrizia's ruthless business dealings, along with her affairs, had placed her in the paparazzi's sights. But it was the discovery of her relationship with a European prince, unearthed by a rookie journalist, that propelled the entire family into the spotlight. Fabrizia had only just turned eighteen when the short-lived affair began. This piece of juicy knowledge added to the relentless media coverage and their desire to sensationalise the events.

For months, fourteen-year-old Sofia had no privacy. She'd been media fodder. Photographers and journalists hounded her. Like her father, she hated attention. He'd arranged for a driver to take her to and from school. Her mother responded with disgust. Fabrizia despised weakness, especially in her own family.

Sofia could remember her parents' arguments clearly.

'Don't let them see it's affecting us,' her mother would scream.

'What do you want from me? To turn my back on her, too?'

Her mother's escalating anger always tore at her father's attempts to stay calm. Most of the time he remained cool. Other times the arguments escalated when he unleashed; his voice booming with frustration.

'She needs to be strong. You don't survive as a woman if you're not strong.'

The Antonelli Corporation was a curse. The bigger the business grew, the colder her mother became. The takeovers and bottom lines strangled all the love out of her parents' marriage. Their finances became the only reason they never divorced.

Her father often escaped to their professionally mani-cured garden to sip a drink and look up at the stars.

'Why do you stay with mama?' Sofia had asked him one night. She curled up next to him as a cool breeze picked up. He wrapped the throw rug around her shoulders and kissed her forehead.

'It is very hard now,' he said sadly. 'The business is too big.'

'I hate her. How she speaks to you. Why do you stay?'

'For you, *mia piccola principessa*.'

Butterflies tickled in Sofia's chest when he called her his little princess. But more like the sword-wielding princes in the fairy tales her nanny read to her, she tried to be her father's shield, protecting him from the criticisms her mother unleashed.

The more Fabrizia grew to despise her husband, the more Sofia loved him and the stronger her resentment grew towards her mother.

All she'd ever wanted to do was protect her father, but Fabrizia had held the family tight with a dominance that it seemed only a magic spell could break.

NOW SHE WAS DEAD.

Ding dong, the witch is dead.

Sofia stopped outside the train station's exit. Shame clawed her insides. Her mother didn't deserve that. And it was pointless anyway. Nothing could change the past, the way her mother acted—not even cruel thoughts.

She shook her head. Even dead, her mother unhinged her.

Midday patrons and day-trippers filled the town's main street. Sofia spotted a taxi idling at the taxi stand. As she made her way along the busy sidewalk, she reminded herself she was no longer the timid child she'd been before leaving Australia. All those years away—building a life in the Tuscan hills, learning Italian, and renovating a three-hundred-year-old villa—had helped her heal.

Ten years ago, Sofia made a choice: shrivel or thrive. She couldn't bear to endure the same fate as her older sisters, who had married dull cardboard cut-outs (the only kind of husband her mother approved of). They ticked all the boxes: sons from wealthy Italian families, who played rugby and rowed in regattas, and earned an obscene amount of money. Her sisters had been groomed since birth to understand the expectations that came with being Fabrizia's daughters. Trust funds would be cut off and credit cards withdrawn, had they chosen to marry men she considered 'beneath' their social standing.

Adriana, the middle sister, was a carbon copy of

Fabrizia. Money and prestige dominated her life. Being married to a successful barrister served its purpose. Sofia, of course, refused to play into Fabrizia's expectations and experienced the financial scorn of her mother. Giulia—her oldest sister and always compliant—didn't know how to go against her mother. For Giulia, life was easier when she agreed and lived the life expected of her.

The clock above the Georgian town hall chimed. Sofia shielded her eyes from the glare that reflected off the steamy blue sky. Midday. She had thirty minutes to change into her funeral outfit and get herself to St Thomas'.

NERVES TANGLED inside the pit of Sofia's stomach. She took a deep breath. She needed to do this. She needed closure.

The service had already started as she crept into a pew at the back of the church. 'Amazing Grace' overlaid the sobering atmosphere. She kept her head down. No one noticed her, their focus pulled towards the mahogany coffin covered in red roses and white lilies.

During the service, Sofia moved her attention from the coffin to her sisters. She could read their emotions from the back. Giulia kept her head on Luca's shoulder. Theirs was a content marriage; she smiled when he placed an arm around her. Unlike Adriana, who sat like the empress of the Southern Highlands. Immaculately dressed, with a large, brimmed hat that announced her wealth and prestige. At one point she thrust a handkerchief at Giulia. Sofia didn't need to see her face to know she was annoyed.

Adriana, like her mother, abhorred any emotion that showed weakness. By her mid-teens, Adriana had grown hard, overpassing Giulia in status despite being younger. Sometimes Sofia wanted to be more like her sisters. But she was neither compliant nor entitled. Instead, she yearned for simplicity. For freedom. For unadulterated love.

When the last hymn began to play, she lost her resolve. She couldn't stomach a scene. Not here. She slipped out and scuttled down the street.

Sofia glanced at the program in her hand. A photo of her mother, still glamorous in her eighties, graced the cover.

'No.' Sofia shook the program. 'You will not win. Not today.'

Sofia let out a harsh breath. An imagined scene played out in her mind where she told her mother about the success she'd had in restoring an old winery in Tuscany. Building a sustainable business. Taking in disenfranchised youth to work at harvest time and give them a purpose. How the way she lived her life fulfilled her need to make a difference in the world.

Her mother's voice jeered. 'You think this is what will bring you success?'

Sofia ripped the program up and released the torn paper to the breeze. Her fingers unclenched and her jaw relaxed as she watched the pieces fly away,

A kookaburra perched on a telegraph pole laughed. Sofia looked up. There was no sign of a storm, but that didn't mean one wasn't coming.

SOFIA EXITED the taxi and tilted the rim of her broad sun hat, hoping its shadow shielded most of her face. A headache had formed behind her eyes on the ride over.

What kind of reception awaited her? She stood at the edge of the mansion's manicured lawn and surveyed the crowd. She recognised many of the guests—all older, extended family, business associates, and friends. It amazed Sofia that her mother had been able to build friendships.

She exhaled and took a step towards the mourners as they pecked at finger food like scavenging crows. No more hiding.

It was Adriana who spotted her first. 'Look what the cat's dragged in.' She twirled a glass of champagne in her hand. 'The prodigal daughter has returned.'

'Hello, Adriana.' The greeting felt like sandpaper in Sofia's mouth.

A sudden cry pulled Sofia away from Adriana's stony stare.

'My goodness, is it really you?'

Sofia allowed herself to be pulled into her eldest sister's arms. 'Hi, Giulia.'

'Let me look at you.' She held Sofia at arm's length. 'You look fabulous. Is it really you?'

'It's me,' Sofia said with a small smile.

The warmth of Giulia's hug lingered, bringing comfort. Her heart surged with love.

Adriana snorted. 'If only we'd known it would take a death to make her resurface, we could've bumped off the old bat years ago.'

'Adriana, don't.' Giulia held Sofia's hand.

Adriana stepped forward, her eyes blazing. 'Or is it because Mum's no longer here? You always were weak—'

Sofia's palm landed hard on Adriana's cheek. The world

stilled, and she felt a flock of eyes upon her. Then the nausea overpowered her, and she ran for the bathroom.

AS SOFIA DRIED the cold water from her face, she glanced around. The marble bathroom with its gilded taps and pear-shaped chandeliers screamed wealth and prestige. Everything her family created was for appearances. The great Italian family: successful migrants who'd come to Australia with nothing, worked hard, and built empires. The Antonellis, wielding their immense success, were symbolic of the lucky country.

Sofia walked through her old home. This had never been a warm house.

Muted chatter and laughter drifted through the open french doors that ran along the entire north side of the house. The sheer curtains billowed, teasing the polished wooden floors. She walked past the master bedroom with its bed cloaked in velvet. Sandalwood furniture was a featured statement. One thing was certain—money bought beautiful rooms. Sofia sighed. What waste. This could've been a wonderful family. What was it all really for?

An unsettling sensation bubbled inside her. Only one room stood out as a place of security and love. Reaching her father's study, she crept inside and closed the door. The cool room immediately offered a refuge. Everything was the same. Her father's precious record collection filled the wooden shelves, their coloured spines like barcodes of listening pleasure. Her father had always told her that the records connected him to his youth and his country of birth. An aural reminder of a simpler, less complicated life.

Sofia followed the records to the record player; the same one she'd known as a child. Purchased at Grace Bros in Sydney, it stood next to the polished teak desk. The player's wooden veneer was a reminder of the days when money was tight—when her father was still building his business, breaking his back to build homes for new migrants. Sometimes she wished for those simpler days. When money wasn't an object in her parents' relationship. Now, in a world obsessed with vintage pieces, the modest record player would fetch a decent price. Sofia smiled at the irony of it and lifted the lid.

Her heart lurched at the sight of the record on the pad: Connie Francis's *Christmas in My Heart*. Her father had died shortly before Christmas. Had he been listening to this when he suffered the stroke?

Sofia turned the power on and placed the needle on the spinning vinyl. The familiar crackle came through the speakers, and then Connie Francis's dulcet tones filled the room. She smiled as she remembered how she would sneak into the study while her father was working on his accounts. She'd tiptoe in and sit under his desk, waiting for his broad hand to rest momentarily on her head. Sometimes she curled into a ball and fell asleep while her father sang along in Italian—the only time she ever heard him speak his native language.

Sofia sifted through the albums and found the one whose cover she loved the most. To a gangly, shy little girl, Connie Francis was the most beautiful woman in the world, with her cheeky side glance and ruby red lips. Dressed in a traditional gondolier's hat and striped top, she was framed by Venice. She made Italy seem romantic and magical.

Sometimes Sofia would close her eyes and pretend that the singer was her mother instead of Fabrizia. She imagined Connie singing her to sleep while her father held her hand.

This was what Sofia had always yearned for—a happy family and a simpler life. Italy had given her a version of this, for Italians lived, breathed, and died according to their motto: *La dolce vita*. The beautiful life. Life was slower. Family and relationships were the focus.

Before settling in Tuscany, she'd spent two years travelling around Italy, picking up work where she could. Venice had been everything she'd imagined. It looked exactly as it had on the album cover. It felt full of life and love. She enjoyed four glorious weeks basking in its history and beauty and stealing passionate kisses from a handsome Italian boy she met in the Gallerie dell'Accademia.

'I thought you'd be in here.' Giulia closed the door behind her and smiled, her eyes twinkling with kindness. Sofia felt a warm sensation in her arms; the shadow touches from where Giulia had embraced her earlier. They had always enjoyed their private moments together.

'You're a little late for Christmas.' Giulia nodded at the record player. 'Want a cognac?'

'Why not.'

Her sister poured a double shot into two cut crystal glasses. She looked older. Not just because Giulia was sixteen years her senior, but because living with Fabrizia drained the life out of you.

Countess Dracula.

'Have you eaten?'

'No.'

'You need to eat. You're way too thin.'

Sofia's heart lurched again. She missed Giulia's maternal ways. Her kindness. Her eldest sister had always looked out for her, stepping in where their mother had failed.

Leaving Giulia, without saying a word to her, had been the hardest decision, but she'd done it out of love. Sofia's departure would be catastrophic to the masquerade her mother projected to the outside world. She would never have been allowed to leave, to damage the happy-family façade—and if it was discovered that Giulia knew about her plans, supported her even, then she would have been cut off too. Sofia couldn't allow that to happen. The guilt she felt when she had slipped from the house in the dead of night, knowing she would break her sister's heart when she woke to find her gone the next day, nearly forced Sofia to turn around. How could she leave sweet Giulia behind to fend for herself against her mother and Adriana? She had carried a deep, regretful sadness inside her ever since.

It was different with Adriana. They were never close. Not that she didn't try. But Adriana's cutting remarks and eye rolling were a constant reminder of how much Sofia annoyed her. She never had the time for her younger sister, swatting Sofia away like an annoying insect. Adriana was the kind of girl who would see her sister's departure as a win for her own selfish needs: one less competitor in the ring.

Giulia passed a glass to Sofia and raised hers in a toast. 'To angry sisters.'

Sofia winced. 'I'm sorry I made a scene. Is Adriana mad?'

Giulia cocked her eyebrow and grinned. 'We wouldn't expect any less.'

A comfortable silence drifted over them as they sipped their drinks.

'I'm glad you came,' Giulia said.

Sofia smiled. She was too. But as she noted the thin

streaks of grey running through Giulia's chestnut hair, sadness seeped in again. The decision to find happiness had cost her ten years with her sister.

'I'm sorry.'

'I know. But Adriana had it coming. I only wish I had the courage to sock her one.' Giulia laughed.

Sofia couldn't help chuckling as well. 'That was some scene. Not very sisterly. It's just—'

'You don't have to say it.'

She knew she did. 'Adriana was right. I ran away. I'm weak.'

'That's not true. We're allowed to feel vulnerable—'

'I was afraid.'

'Of Adriana?'

'No, Mum.'

'Oh.' Giulia swirled the liquid in her glass. 'You know, she wasn't always so hard.'

'Sure fooled me. That certainly wasn't my experience.'

'No, really.'

Tinkling bells came through the speakers and Connie Francis's 'Have Yourself a Merry Little Christmas' filled the room. Sofia smiled. 'She did love Christmas, didn't she? All the "Santa is coming tonight" charade when I was little.'

'She liked to spoil you.' Giulia propped her legs on the coffee table.

'You know, I never let on that I had stopped believing in Santa Claus for a few years after I found out. I didn't want to lose Christmas Mum. She was different. Warmer. Looking back, it's the only time she was truly decent.'

Giulia reached across and squeezed Sofia's hand. 'What you got was damaged. I remember her laughter, how it filled the house.'

'Why did it stop?' Sofia asked, even though she knew the answer.

'Money, greed, power. I don't know. Take your pick.'

'When Dad died—' Sofia swallowed hard and fought back tears. 'When he died, it devastated me.' She let the tears fall. 'You weren't here, Giulia. You got to go home. Both of you did. To husbands who loved you.' Sofia's voice cracked. 'I was alone. I had no one.'

'You were always welcome to stay with us.'

Sofia shrugged. 'Maybe.' She got up and drained the cognac. 'The truth is, I was scared and so unhappy. It was awful alone in the house with Mum. Dad gone. You and Adriana married. Seeing what you had made me feel worse. I wasn't like you and Adriana. I felt trapped. Plus, I always felt I never belonged. If it wasn't for that Demi Moore-style photo of her pregnant with me, I'd think I was adopted.' She let out a dry chuckle.

Tears filled Giulia's eyes. They'd all been hurt in some way. Maybe Adriana was hurting too. The three of them were so different. They would handle hurt differently, too. Mum had been hard on all of them. Not in the same way, but it hurt just the same. Sophia sighed. She'd been too hard on Adriana. She needed to be kinder to her. Be the better person.

'Why did you come back?' Giulia asked softly.

'Because she was still my mother. I'd never forgive myself if I didn't. I didn't want her to not exist. I know all too well how that feels.' Sofia refilled her glass. 'Adriana was right. I was weak. I should've stood up for what I wanted. Not feared Mum's disappointment. In the end I proved her right, didn't I? By running off. Not making contact for years.' She took a long gulp of cognac and swirled the amber liquid around her tongue, relishing the burn as she swallowed. 'Now I need to move forward. To be kind to myself.'

They sat in comfortable silence, listening to the wake outside. Children playing. People laughing. A baby crying. Life.

'Giulia—'

'I know. I can see it etched all over your face. You're not staying.'

Sofia sighed and shook her head. 'No.'

'Well, you're braver than you think, little sister. How long will you be staying?'

'A few weeks?'

'Okay, I'll take that.'

'Will Adriana?'

'She'll come around ... eventually. Or you can slap some more sense into her.'

'Very funny.' Sofia laughed. It felt good.

Giulia got up. 'I suppose we can't hide in here forever. Meet you out in the garden?'

'Sure, just give me a sec. Thanks, Giulia.'

'Anytime.'

Sofia moved to the record player, stopped the record and removed it, then slid it back into its cover. 'Is it okay if I take this?'

'Sure.' Giulia blew her a kiss and closed the door softly behind her.

Sofia reached up and grasped her locket tight in her hand. She was glad she had fought her demons to come back. No matter how fractured, Giulia and Adriana were still family. If there was anything she'd learned from living in Italy, it was that family was important.

Sofia felt her phone vibrate in her jacket. She smiled as she looked at the call display.

'*Ciao, dolcezza.* Are you being good for papa? ... *Va bene*, good ... Yes, Frannie, Mummy misses you too.'

She opened the locket. A photo of her daughter, caught in a moment of joy, looked back at her with unconditional love. Everything would be okay. Frannie was her world. The greatest gift of love. Time was her gift to her daughter, and she had plenty to give.

THE BLESSING

The car swerved into the driveway and came to an abrupt stop.

Corinna's fingers were cramped from gripping the seatbelt for the duration of the erratic trip across town. She glanced at her mother, who sat in the driver's seat, pushing out sharp bursts of air from her mouth. A deep frown creased her forehead.

Corinna's stomach filled with dread, and she braced herself for the barrage of words to come.

'Why, Corinna?' Tired, disappointed eyes glared at her.

There was nothing Corinna could say. She lacked the responses her mother wanted to hear. She knew she'd been moody, cruel.

It was as if someone else had possessed her. Corinna worried about it constantly. Would her confident, happy self ever find its way out again? Or had some sinister curse descended upon her permanently, chaining her to a sullen imprisonment? Some days she woke with a pulsating irritation. On those days, she craved to punch the world in the face.

'Well?' Her mother waited.

Corinna sunk into the seat. 'I don't know.' She let the sound of the blinker's monotonous clicking drown out her mother's growing frustration and turned to look out of the window at her grandmother's front yard, filled to the brim with shrubs.

Her gaze travelled the stony path to the front door waiting to intern her. Punishment for all the lies and dishonesty. A raw hurt at being abandoned by her mother stabbed at her heart.

Her mother killed the engine and opened the car door. 'Let's go.'

Corinna let out a long, purposeful sigh. This was ridiculous. What did her mum want from her? To die of boredom for the next two weeks?

With force, her mother pulled the door closed again. 'I don't understand you anymore.'

Corinna whirled around to face her mother for a verbal battle. But what she saw knocked her off-kilter: silent tears trickling down her mum's cheeks. She wanted to wipe them away. Tell her she was sorry. For all of it. Instead, she stayed silent, her arms crossed tight across her chest. She stared at the peeling paint on the terrace house and swallowed the lump in her throat.

'Sorry.' The apology came out hard and sarcastic. She cringed, immediately regretting it.

As expected, this detonated her mother. 'I beg your pardon?!'

The punitive tone triggered Corinna's own rage. 'I *said* I was *sorry*. Geez!' The words came out cold and vicious.

Slap!

Pinpricks of light danced across her vision.

Corinna's desire to grab her mother's greying ponytail

and rip it from her scalp was balanced by a desire to hug her and apologise. She embraced her nastier side.

'Fuck off.'

'Get out.'

'No.'

'Just get out. Nonna is waiting for you.'

'Mum—'

'I don't want to look at you. I don't want to speak with you.'

'Why are you being so mean?' Corinna couldn't stop her voice from cracking.

Her mother closed her eyes and started whispering something in her Sicilian dialect, like a mantra of protection against her own daughter. When she finished, she squeezed the evil eye that hung on a silver chain on the rear view mirror. The blue bead with its black eye glared back at Corinna. Judging her.

'Are you putting a hex on me?' Corinna lifted her chin in defiance. Her chest thumped in response at the cruel question. Why couldn't she just keep her mouth shut?

Her mother sighed, started the car, and waited in silence for Corinna to leave. Corinna knew it was no use. Her mother's silent treatment hurt just as much as the slap.

'Fine.'

Corinna yanked her bag from the back seat and got out of the car. She stormed past her nonna, who stood at the gate, took the stairs two at a time, and landed on the porch in a tangle of emotions. This was so embarrassing. What if the girls at school found out her strict Italian mother forced her to stay at her grandmother's? Just great. More ammo to add to the 'wog lunch' and twangy accent comments. Being called 'Pizza Rizzo' because of her surname.

Corinna clenched her hands and let out an angry sigh.

Most of the time it was fun banter, but it turned up the spotlight even more. She envied the class roll with all the Anglo names. She longed to be a Jones, Sullivan, or Moore. Her short frame, mop of black curls, and olive skin was no competition to her taller and fairer peers. They had sprawling friendship groups and moved between each other's houses after school, fitting in perfectly with the casual routine of dinnertime. They were allowed to go to slumber parties, parties with boys, and the city at night. Her life was dictated by archaic 1950s expectations.

From the veranda, she tried to listen to her grandmother and mother talking. Fractured phrases, spoken in Italian, floated up to her. 'She'll be okay ... Don't worry ... She knows you love her.' In Italian, the words sound like prayers of hope. This only added to Corinna's guilt.

She watched her mother's car drive away and waited hesitantly at the front door.

Nonna smiled and patted Corinna's hand. '*Andiamo*. Come. I will show you the bed to sleep in.'

Duffle bag in hand, Corinna shadowed her grandmother into the house. The delicious aroma of garlic and onions seduced her senses, distracting her from her distress. From the belly of the house, Italian music playing on a radio. Corinna cringed at the sound of an accordion playing.

Photographs covered the cool, dark walls of the hallway. Corinna took in the images entombed in an eclectic array of frames. Images of people from the past. Some of the frames had dried palm fronds tucked behind them, reverently marking the passing of loved ones. Nonna understood the sacredness of the palms. Every year, she made each of them come home from Palm Sunday mass with a palm frond: they needed to be kept with respect and reverence. Her mother kept theirs in a box in the hall cupboard with some of her father's things.

Nonna led Corinna into the room that would be her bedroom for the next two weeks—her entire school holiday. She surveyed the outdated little room. A crocheted bedspread and embroidered pillowcases dressed a heavy wooden bed. A silver amulet was nailed to the bedhead. Corinna ran her fingers over it. Branches sprouting. At the end of each branch sat a symbol: a blossom, a key, the moon, and a dagger.

'This looks medieval. What is it?'

'*Una cimaurta.*' Nonna stood next to Corinna. 'It is old belief.' She placed a warm hand on Corinna's cheek. 'To take away evil.'

A sense of ease flowed through her at Nonna's touch, tempering the resentment she'd harboured since her mother declared her punishment.

'Come. Hang your clothes here.'

Nonna opened an old-fashioned wardrobe, releasing a waft of rosemary and sandalwood.

Corinna walked over and placed her bag inside.

'*Va bene*. Very well.' The old woman took Corinna's hands and gazed gently at her. Her faded eyes overflowed with kindness. 'It will be okay. You see. You put things away and come have some coffee.'

Corinna felt tears well up. She swallowed and nodded. Nonna always made her feel loved, no matter what she did or said.

As her nonna left, Corinna sat heavily on the bed and studied the portrait of the Virgin Mary on the wall. She was draped in a royal blue fabric. It was a gentle image of a young mother gazing down at her sleeping baby. Jesus's chubby little hand lay upon her chest. The image made Corinna's heart ache.

She hated this friction with her mum, but she held any love for her hostage, along with every other emotion that made her feel fragile and unstable. It was all she knew how to do now.

It hadn't always been like this. She remembered how, when she was younger, her mother taught her to make pancakes. She'd laughed when Corinna spilled flour all over the place. Had made smiley faces in the mess with her finger.

Where had it all unravelled? And why?

Corinna knew why. Or rather, because of whom.

Julie Scott.

SHE'D JOINED Immaculata College in year ten, after the summer holidays. Julie embodied everything Corinna wished she could be. Lithe and blue-eyed, she had a soft smattering of freckles across her pale skin and a perfect fringe—no stubborn cowlick in sight. Julie was the quintessential Aussie teenager. She looked like the models who graced the cover of *Girlfriend* magazine.

From the moment Mrs Templeton introduced them and asked Corinna to look after Julie, Corinna wanted to be exactly like her. Julie was so confident. She stood up to the teachers and didn't let the cool girls intimidate her. Where Corinna never dared to walk through the area they sat in for lunch, Julie didn't care. She purposely marched through, ignoring their catty remarks and waving away the pungent clouds of cigarette smoke they blew at her. Once, she abruptly turned to declare, 'You know ladies, smoking will give you a cat's bum mouth.' She pouted her lips before sauntering off laughing.

Corinna didn't have any close friends at school. The girls she sat with were like ghosts. They existed but no one really took any notice of them. They did what they were told and never put themselves in the spotlight. For Corinna, they were social props so she didn't feel like a loser. By sitting with them, she didn't stick out—who would pay attention to the lanky Italian girl eating left-over lasagne, or prosciutto and provolone sandwiches when quieter girls were sitting either side of her.

She constantly recorded her voice into her smartphone, playing it back as she listened then worked at softening her vowels, to make them rounder.

The friendship with Julie flourished in an instant. Julie loved that she was Italian.

'I don't know why you're so worried. Everyone bangs on about going out to Italian restaurants. Drinking Italian wine.' She looked over to where the cool girls sat in a huddle. 'I bet they all own designer clothes and shoes made in Italy. They're just jealous.'

These comments cemented her admiration of Julie. She copied everything her new friend did.

After her dad's death, Corinna's mother had become strict and protective, but Julie had a way with her—she was always able to convince her to let Corinna do things she would never have agreed to in the past.

Under Julie's wing, Corinna learned to wag school and sneak off to the beach, where they'd meet boys. Julie smoked pot and encouraged Corinna to join her. Mints, Victoria's Secret body spray, and eyedrops became essential items.

'Spray it in your hair and wash your hands,' Julie reminded Corinna before she headed home.

Corinna started lying all the time. Going to parties instead of the movies. Hanging out with boys instead of being at the shops. It was scary at first but then the adrenaline became addictive. Exciting things were happening in her life, and she loved having others laugh at what her and Julie got up to. Boys were beginning to take an interest in her too. No longer did Corinna worry her life was as bland and boring as the scuffed beige walls in the school corridors: everything was thrumming with new, neon colours.

Then it all came crashing down. Corinna agreed to that age-old teenage scam for the sake of a music festival. 'You say I'm sleeping at your house, and I'll say I'm staying at your house,' Julie had said, stuffing a sequin top into her bag.

At the festival, tipsy on booze bought with a fake ID, Corinna hooked up with a boy who'd showered her with compliments. She loved every minute of their mosh-pit make-out session until a firm hand landed on her shoulder and pulled them apart.

The blood drained from her veins when she found herself face-to-face with her older cousin Tony.

'What the hell are you doing here?'

He stepped forward and sniffed at Corinna. 'You've been drinking? And you stink like an ashtray.'

'Please don't tell Mum,' Corinna begged.

'No can do.' He grabbed Corinna and dragged her away. 'What were you thinking? This isn't a place for fifteen-year-olds! You've totally crossed the line.'

Her mother was livid when Tony deposited her on the doorstep. And in a flood of fear, her every deception tumbled out. The banishment to Nonna's house was her mother's calculated move to sever Julie's influence. But the biggest blow had been learning she was a pawn in Julie's game. She wasn't the only shy girl Julie had befriended to join her on escapades and manipulate for her own purposes. The Immaculata College was Julie's third school.

Julie's deception had been crushing. Corinna winced with shame at the thought of her blind faith and stupidity.

Her nonna knocked and entered. '*Voi un café con biscotti.*'

Corinna nodded. The smell of percolating coffee made her stomach rumble. She trailed Nonna into the bright and cosy kitchen. A collection of mortars and pestles stood drying on a tea towel on the bench. Jars of herbs and spices sat in a rack. All labelled in Italian.

Nonna's knitting sat on her rocking chair in the sitting room, a little area that jutted out from the kitchen. The room added to the cosiness of the kitchen and looked out into the garden. Nonna's sewing machine stood in the corner, a pile of clothes folded on the chair next to it. Corinna's heart lurched; Nonna still took in sewing to help support her pension. An assortment of kitschy knick-knacks adorned a wooden dresser that took up most of the space. Corinna smiled. When she was little, she yearned to play with the porcelain animals. But Nonna always covered it with a sheet to ward off sticky, inquisitive hands.

Corinna sat at the old kitchen table, bought decades ago when her grandparents first migrated from Italy.

Nonna placed the coffee and the biscuits, still warm from the oven, in front of Corinna. 'Eat.' She sat opposite her.

Corinna could no longer control her tears, and a few

trickled down her cheeks. Nonna's mothering pried open her embarrassment and remorse. Deep down, Corinna knew what she'd done was unfair. She'd made things even harder for her mum, who was still mourning her father. Corinna sniffed and wiped the tears with the back of her hand. Nonna had every right to be angry—Mum was her youngest and they were close—but instead, she offered kindness and warmth.

Her nonna sat and waited with unruffled patience. '*Perche*? Why, Corinna? Why did you do all this?'

The question, asked with sincerity, fortified a little trust in Corinna. 'I've always felt so different.'

Nonna smiled and reached across the table to take her hand.

'I'm ashamed of being Italian,' Corinna blurted. Saying it out loud unleashed a torrent of tears. 'I just wanted to fit in.'

Nonna stood. 'Come.'

Corinna wiped her tears on her sleeve and followed her out into the garden. Colourful plants and herbs grew in garden beds. A thicket of rose bushes framed a mismatched hen house made from old wooden doors. Tucked in the corner, under the shade of a frangipani tree, stood a quaint little shed. Wind chimes sang above the door. Butterflies, bees, and dragonflies hovered around the plants. She watched the fat brown hens clucking with delight as they scratched for food in the dark soil and marvelled at this little backyard oasis brimming with flowers and greenery.

Nonna was waiting for Corinna to catch up.

'Don't the chickens dig up your flowers?' she asked. Her dad had tried to raise chooks but had given up when they destroyed her mother's garden.

Nonna grinned. 'No. I give them special medicine in their food and say an old prayer. *Un incanto.*'

Corinna's eyes widened. 'Like a spell?'

It made sense, she supposed. Nonna was always chanting something as she mixed herbs with tea—the tea that tasted different and always made her feel better when she had period pain or a headache.

Nonna patted her hand, smiled, and disappeared inside the little shed. Corinna followed and inhaled an assortment of scents—rose petals, lavender, and other spicy, unusual fragrances. Bundles of dried herbs covered the ceiling. The windowsill housed several strange-looking plants in pots. Mortars and pestles, in all shapes and sizes, sat on a wooden bench next to a bundle of old leatherbound books. Corinna opened one volume and turned the yellowing pages. Verses in Italian filled each page.

A clock chimed. On top of the bookcase stood a clock with two rings, one smaller than the other. Symbols she recognised from astrology charts ran around the smaller ring. Astrological symbols ran around the inner circle. The hand with a silver bauble sat still at her star sign, Aquarius. The clock didn't follow the traditional twelve hours. Roman numerals circled the larger perimeter.

'What kind of clock is this?'

'*Un orologio astromomico,*' Nonna said with a shrug. 'An old clock I use with the herbs.'

'The numbers around the edge are different.' Corinna counted twenty-four.

'It tells old Italian hours.'

'Like twenty-four-hour time.'

'*Si.* You are a clever girl, Corinna.'

Corinna watched Nonna place dried leaves and flowers into a small linen bag. The woman then muttered hushed phrases in a dialect Corinna didn't recognise. Her skin prickled as an energy stirred within the shed.

'*Andiamo.*' Nonna's command broke the stillness.

Corinna stepped outside, letting her eyes adjust to the sunshine. She felt calmer.

Behind her, her grandmother locked the door with an old key, kissed it, then placed it in the pocket of her apron. She sat on the stone bench nestled among the rose bushes and tapped the vacant part of the seat, inviting Corinna to sit next to her.

Corinna did as requested. A warm breeze stirred, and she turned her face upwards, relishing the sunshine and the sweet air.

Nonna placed the small linen bag into her hands.

Corinna lifted it to her nose. She detected the smell of rose petals among pungent herbs. 'What's this for?'

'This will help you find peace.' Nonna reached inside her apron pocket and pulled out a gold necklace with two charms.

'The evil eye will protect you from bad spirits and the cornetto will help bring great love for Italia and your heritage. They will make you strong—make you who you were born to be.'

Nonna murmured a prayer-like chant as she clasped the pendant around Corinna's neck. 'You must be kind to where you come from. It is what makes you *una ragazza forte*. A strong girl.' She kissed her with tenderness on each cheek and picked up the basket filled with cut herbs. 'I am going to make lunch now. You come and help? S*i?*'

'Yes.' Corinna smiled at her grandmother. She touched the two ornaments and closed her eyes. For the first time in a long while, a feeling of quiet contentment moved through her. Her anger and irritation disappeared. All her insecurities drifted away, magically dissolving into nothing.

Magic!

Corinna opened her eyes. 'Nonna, are you—?'

But Nonna was already halfway down the path.

She smiled. A lightness surged through her as the peaceful contentment pushed some of the darkness away.

BEFORE AND AFTER

The River

Helena

Lightning split the dark sky in two. I ducked low. The summer storm had hit with ferocity. Desperate to get to the jetty, I braced myself for the boom to follow and carried on. The rain whipped against my cotton dress, now drenched and heavy against my body.

How was I going to explain this to my parents? I was supposed to be in my room, not running towards the river. Panic surged me forward.

EXCITEMENT FROLICKED INSIDE ME. I tried to contain the jittery feeling in my chest while helping Mum with the dishes. As soon as the kitchen was gleaming, I'd be free.

I was confident my parents suspected nothing. The

deception had been easy so far. Although a hard nugget of guilt sat in the pit of my stomach, it would disappear when I saw Leo. Later, I'd sneak back into my bedroom through the french doors that opened on the veranda and they'd be none the wiser.

Until a week ago, I'd been the dutiful Greek daughter, having learned at an early age that it was easier to accept the rules than to fight them. I attended church and helped my mother host Sunday lunch afterwards. I went to Greek school with no complaints and did my chores when expected. My only friends were those my parents liked: studious, quiet, and happy to come to my house to watch movies or swim in the pool. Some of my Greek cousins and friends battled with their parents about going to parties, what they wore, even what subjects they wanted to study. Their lives were messy, filled with emotional turmoil, fights, and frustration. It was just easier to play the compliant daughter—until I could live my own life.

Independent life was nearly within my grasp. I'd been accepted into an arts law program at Sydney University. In March, I'd leave Grafton and live freely in a big city. I could see my older brother Joey whenever I wanted. God, I missed him. Before he moved away, my brother had accompanied me to and from school, or tagged along when I went with friends to the movies or the mall. He would turn a blind eye and keep a discreet distance when boys came over to chat to us and his respect meant everything to me.

Dad entered the kitchen, shaking the wet out of his greying hair.

'You're soaked.' I handed him a dry tea towel. 'And you're making puddles on Mum's clean floor.' I threw him another tea towel.

'The storm's knocked out the lights on the jetty.' He stamped his feet and hung up his raincoat.

I swallowed a lump of worry. That might be an issue for Leo. He used the lights on the jetty to guide him in, where I waited for him, underneath the walkway. He'd been to visit me every night over the past week.

The jetty was our property's *pièce de résistance*. As kids, my brother, cousins and I would race each other from the back door, hot-footing down the cobbled path until we landed on the worn timbers. The jetty would creak and moan under our weight until we bombed ourselves into the expansive river. We'd let the tide take us downstream, floating on our backs, the sun tickling our exposed faces. The swim back against the tide shaped us into strong and capable swimmers. My brother and I always made the regionals during our school swimming carnivals. Each summer our fitness increased as we raced each other across the one-kilometre return distance, from our jetty and back again.

Now that I was all grown up, the jetty brought me new delights.

Once my parents were glued to the TV, I announced that I was going to my room to read. I kissed my parents goodnight, and my heart pounded with such strength I worried they'd see it through my dress.

Minutes later, I slipped out through the french doors as I had done every night this week. An eerie sky roiled above me, filled with indigo clouds against steel grey. The rain, having eased for a moment, started up again, almost as if in protest—a warning to not venture out.

I shoved my phone in the back pocket of my dress, slid on my gumboots, and sprinted down to the jetty. My plastic rain jacket fluttered out behind me as conflicting desires battled in my mind. I wanted nothing more than to see Leo, but I hoped he hadn't ventured out in this weather.

By the time I reached the jetty, the rain was falling in unyielding sheets, snatching away all visibility.

'Leo!' I called over and over. Each time, the wind caught his name and carried it away.

My hands shook as I grabbed my phone and turned on the torch.

'Leo!'

The storm sniggered at the pathetic scrap of light—a weak beacon.

Panic gripped my chest as I ran down to the water's edge. I scanned the river with controlled precision.

Nothing.

Relief, laced with disappointment, washed over me and lodged itself in my heart. He'd decided not to come. It would have been our last night together before he headed back to Sydney with his mates.

Then I saw it. A swollen red belly rocking on the thrashing waves.

Horror shook me. Leo's rowboat. It had capsized.

My adrenaline detonated, and I ran towards the family tinny thrashing at its mooring. My gumboot slipped on the aluminium ladder and I fell, hitting the middle of my back on the edge of the seat. The wind was knocked out of me; I lay there in searing pain.

I needed to calm down. To stop the rising panic.

Ignoring the sharp pain that spasmed in my lower back, I forced myself up. I placed a foot against the edge of the boat and yanked the cord to start the motor. The tinny bucked and pounded in the relentless wind. I pulled until my arms ached.

'Come on!' I screamed. As if hearing my desperation,

the little motor spluttered to life. 'Yes!' I threw off the rope, twisted the throttle, and the boat reared into action. The smell of petrol choked me as I gunned the engine.

I reached the capsized boat. I circled around it but couldn't see anything.

Leo. No, no, no

My hands shook as I called triple zero. For a moment, all I heard was a barrage of noise on the other end. My brain caught up and I realised someone was asking me questions.

'Do you require police, fire, or ambulance?'

'I ... I don't know! My friend's fallen out of his boat. He's missing in the Clarence River!'

'I'll connect you to the police.'

A new voice came over the phone. But the words didn't register.

I'd spotted him. His body had fallen onto the upturned propeller, keeping part of his head above the waterline.

Without hesitating, I stripped down to my underpants and dove into the rocking river. I swam towards Leo with desperate, determined strokes.

Please be alive.

The Festival

Helena

THE BARMAN HAD FINALLY SPOTTED me in the throng. He came over, placed both hands on the counter, and gave me a cheeky wink. 'What can I get you?'

'I don't know. I've never had a drink before.' I leaned over the bar that ran along the entire side of the old wool shearer's shed. The polished red timber reflected the coloured string lights that hung above.

He raised a pierced eyebrow.

'I've just turned eighteen,' I shouted over the laughter and chatter in the bar. The vibrant energy thrilled me.

'What? You mean, never had alcohol?'

I shook my head.

'Not even a sneaky one at a party?'

'I wasn't allowed to go to parties.'

The barman's face creased with surprise. He was good-looking in a gritty, weathered sort of way. His arms were covered in intricate tattoos—a stark contrast to my fair, skinny arms.

A group of girls congregated next to me, jostling me where I sat perched on a stool. Their confidence was over-powering as they tried to get the barman's attention. They laughed through pouted red lips and fluttered thick, over-sized eyelashes that reminded me of furry caterpillars.

'Sorry,' one of them said, glancing at me. She flicked her long blonde hair. 'Did we cut in?'

'No.' I avoided eye contact with the girl as I shrunk back on my stool. My sensible denim shorts and yellow checked shirt, tied loosely in a knot at the front, were no competition for their crop tops and shorts that barely covered their bottoms. I realised there was a festival dress code that I hadn't been made aware of—less fabric and more flesh.

I played with the coaster on the bar and waited.

'You're a regular Cinderella,' the barman moved away from the girls and stood in front of me again. He shot a look of thanks at a girl with facial piercings who took his place and began to make their drink order. I smiled as the girls muttered their disappointment at being ignored.

'Except I came in my cousin's Jeep, instead of a magic pumpkin. I do need to be home by midnight, though.' I mentally high-fived myself at my witty response. Being noticed by a good-looking barman was helping me relax.

'Well, we better get you a drink then. How about a beer?' He flicked the tops of the broad silver taps in front of me. Fat Yak, Stone and Wood, 150 Lashes—all names that had nothing to do with beer.

'I don't know. You choose.'

He opened the fridge behind him, grabbed a bottle of Little Creatures and cracked it open.

'On the house. Happy eighteenth.'

'Thanks.' I smiled shyly and took a tentative sip. It was bitter but also citrusy and sweet.

The girls next to me gasped collectively. I turned to see what was causing them to hyperventilate. I should have known.

Alex.

'There you are,' he said to me, ignoring the attention. The gaggle of girls started to flap their hands and whimper.

'I'm supposed to be keeping an eye on you.'

'I'm good,' I said with a giggle. 'I'm having my first beer.'

He grinned. 'Listen, sorry about leaving you, but I have to go with the boys. We have some interviews and other stuff before we're due on. Will you be okay?'

'I'll be fine. I promise.'

'Are you sure?'

'Yep. You can stop being so protective. I'm fine. I'm not that scrawny kid anymore, Al. But then, neither are you!' I poked at his stomach teasingly. 'Too much rock star food. I could beat you in a race down the river any day.'

Alex laughed. 'You wish.'

The girls behind him started to snap photos on their smartphones. Alex turned his back further, blocking them and hiding me from view.

'I promised to look out for you. I want my best-nephew status to be intact when I drop you home.' He nudged me. 'In one piece.'

'Go.' I shoved him back. 'There's heaps of security. I have my phone and my pass to get backstage if I need to. Unless—' I waved the pass at him, '—I sell it to some crazy fans for top dollar.' I threw him a mischievous grin.

Alex mimed a knife going through his heart. Some bloke in the bar called out, 'Hey Alex!' He looked around. Uncertainty wiped his smile away.

'You sure?'

'She'll be right, I'll keep an eye on her.' The barman handed me a bag of chips.

'See?' I kissed Alex on the cheek, revelling at the reaction from the girls. 'I'll be fine. Now *go*.'

I watched patrons nudge each other, their mouths gaping in awe, as the lead guitarist from Modest Thrones sauntered past them out of the bar, throwing me one last look as he left. The girls next to me had gone into a tailspin. Standing centimetres away from a member of the hottest band in the country had them shrieking. I suddenly didn't feel so bad about being a Pollyanna.

'So, your cousin's Alex Stamos.' The barman smiled.

'Yeah. He *did* go to parties.' I laughed and sipped my beer.

Leo

SHE WAS a breath of fresh air among the groupies. *Different from the other girls.* I cringed as the soppy cliché entered my thoughts.

We'd been lucky to find a place to sit not too far from the bar. The five of us crammed our stools around it. Every time one of us knocked the table legs, empty beer glasses rang out in protest. The place was crowded and noisy. People were in great spirits. My mates were too busy bantering about conquests and footy results and rating the bands to notice my focus was elsewhere. Like everyone, I'd been curious when Alex from Modest Thrones walked into the bar. It was unusual for a rock star to enter the domain of common punters. But I'd been more interested in the girl he'd been talking to.

God, there was something special about her. A warm feeling flowed through me as I watched her laugh with Scott. Then she twisted around on the stool, and her gaze met mine. All the air rushed out of my lungs. She smiled and I smiled back and, without thinking, mouthed, 'Hi.'

She lobbed a gentle hello back, and the pit of my stomach stirred.

Scott caught my eye and waved me over. I jumped at the opportunity and left my mates arguing over the State of Origin selection.

'G'day, Leo.' Scott cracked open my usual—a bottle of Canadian Club—and slid it over to me. 'Whatcha think of the bands this year?'

'Yeah, it's a good lineup. Best in years. I can't believe they got the Modest Thrones to play.' I flicked a look at the girl. She seemed to be concentrating on sipping her beer. 'Wasn't that Alex Stamos who just walked in here?'

Scott directed his attention to the girl. 'Yep, he's ... sorry, I didn't get your name?'

'Helena.'

She seemed unpretentious. She had this natural way about her. The way she smiled—her face beamed with kindness and her hazel eyes sparkled under the lights. Goosebumps rippled down my neck and my heart thrummed.

'Alex is Helena's cousin.'

'He caused a bit of stir.' I sipped my drink.

'Yeah,' she said with a chuckle. 'He does that. At home, too.'

'So, Helena, eh? The face that launched a thousand ships,' I said.

'Sorry?' Scott looked at me as if I'd just said the lamest thing.

But Helena beamed. 'That's what my *yiayia* says.'

'Greek mythology,' we said at the same time, and laughed. A connection.

I extended my hand. 'My name's Leo.'

She took it, her hand sitting warm and fragile inside mine. I noticed how petite she was up close. 'Nice to meet you. How did you get into Greek mythology?'

'I studied it in my first year of architecture at uni. I loved it when I was a kid, too. All those gods wielding power.'

'Helena here has just turned eighteen.' Scott winked at me, and I gave him the look.

Taking the hint, he walked off to help Freya serve the group of giggly girls. Helena was such a contrast to their over-made, pouty faces. Plastic-looking girls who flocked and flapped around like a bunch of cockatoos shrieking at each other.

I slid onto the stool next to her, trying to act nonchalant. 'What do you think of the bands this year?' I turned the glass on the paper coaster, nerves pulsating throughout my body.

'This is actually my first music festival.' She cleared her throat and picked at the label on her empty beer bottle. She seemed a little nervous. 'My parents are Greek. Strict. Alex has a gift for getting his own way, and he talked my parents into letting me come with him. Though they'd die if they knew I was sitting in a bar, having a beer and talking to boys.'

That made sense. I'd heard Alex talk about his Greek heritage on a podcast, describing the hard slog of convincing his family that playing in a rock band wasn't the demon job they'd proclaimed.

'This is my first beer, too.' She lifted the bottle.

I smiled. I remembered the feeling of having my first legal beer when I turned eighteen, six years ago.

'Well, let me buy you another one,' I said, hoping to prolong the conversation. I loved her openness. 'Have you seen any of the other bands?'

'Yep, but everyone gets so hyped up, I get jostled and stepped on. I needed a break.' She paused then leaned forward. 'Some guy put his hand on my bum and squeezed it. It freaked me out. So I came in here.'

A primal protectiveness flooded through me. It pissed me off, knowing some bloke out there was giving the rest of us a bad name.

She continued before I could say anything. 'It's okay though. If I tell Alex, he'll make me stay backstage. I really want to experience it all from the front.'

'How about I go out there with you? I mean, if you want.' I shrugged and glanced away, but my heart was racing. 'No pressure.'

I hoped I didn't sound like a dick. But looking at Helena again, I relaxed a little. She had a sincerity that made me feel at ease.

'Really? Are you sure?'

'Why not? It'll be my good deed for the day.'

'That'd be great.' Her smile radiated through me. 'But ...' She bit her bottom lip. 'I'll take you up on that drink offer first, if that's okay?' She rested her cheek in her hand and looked straight at me. 'I mean, if you're going to be my body-guard, I should know all your dark secrets.'

I laughed. 'Sure. But I'll warn you, all my secrets are boring.'

'Just how I like them.' Helena nudged me.

I was hooked.

Helena

'ARE you sure you want to watch the last band of the night with *me* and not your mates?' I glanced over my shoulder at Leo's friends. They were all grinning at us. Leo and I had been talking for over an hour, and I'd just looked at my watch. Quarter to seven. The Modest Thrones were due to come on.

'Nah, I've spent enough time with those losers. Happy to have some decent company for a change.' Leo smirked. 'Besides, those VIP tickets will keep my arse safe from the screaming girls out there.'

I loved his cheeky sense of humour. And that smile. He was great company and made me feel so at ease—nothing like the immature the boys I knew. They only swooned over girls who looked like they'd stepped out of a filtered Instagram post.

As we talked, I'd uncovered Leo's intelligence and wit. The best thing was his genuine interest in my Greek culture. He ticked all the boxes—and he was good-looking, too. Every time he laughed, his blue eyes flashed with joy.

He guided me off the stool and escorted me out of the bar. My heart skipped a beat when he touched my arm. I couldn't wait to enjoy some music and watch Alex bring his guitar to life. I wanted to experience the moment with Leo. There was a connection I couldn't ignore.

Leo

DUSK HAD SETTLED IN, and the bright lights that framed the stage glowed against the sweeping oranges and reds of the summer sunset. Helena had cheered and sung through every song. She was mesmerising. I loved watching her face light up as the rhythm of the music swept over her. Her excitement captivated me. I could also see her brimming with pride.

Modest Thrones had been my favourite band for a while. That's why I'd changed my plans at the last minute. I'd originally arranged to spend the weekend working on house plans for a customer who couldn't decide whether they wanted a sunken lounge room. But I ended up here instead, and fate had given me a gift.

Maybe it was the music. Maybe it was the balmy summer's evening. Maybe it was because Helena had grabbed my hand. Regardless of the reason, I knew I'd fallen hard. I cringed at the naff phrase that floated into my mind, but I felt the truth of the words—Helena was my soulmate. I shook my head and laughed.

'What's so funny?' she asked.

'Nothing. I was just thinking about how much fun I'm having.'

'Me too. Thanks for being my bodyguard.' She stood on her tiptoes and kissed my cheek. Her face flushed and she looked down, as if afraid she'd overstepped.

I moved her in front of me and wrapped my arms around her, our fingers interlacing. I wouldn't let Helena go.

The River

Helena

SEARCHLIGHTS SKITTERED across the surface of the water. The rain hadn't let up. The cold droplets stung my face and forearms as my strength slowly seeped out of me. My arms were screaming. I was gripping the boat's motor with one hand to keep us afloat, and propping Leo's head above water in the crook of my other arm. I didn't know how long I had been holding us like this, anchoring us against the fast-moving current. My teeth chattered. My knuckles were white as they gripped Leo's sodden shirt. Numbness had claimed every extremity.

'Hang on!' I kept shouting at Leo. 'Please.'

I wept. Our time hadn't even begun. Only a few stolen kisses. I hadn't wanted to rush into anything, and Leo understood.

Despite terror fuelling my death grip on him, he was

slipping out of my hands. The watery fingers of the river were easing him away from me and I was so, so tired. I couldn't hold on any longer. My tears mixed with the rain but I had no strength to cry out. My vision blurred.

Out of the dark, wet abyss, I felt a pair of hands reach out and grab Leo. Then another pair grabbed me.

BETRAYAL

I swerve onto the motorway, triggering the blasting of a car horn and a middle finger from someone to my right. I shoot one in return.

My grandmother's gentle voice plays in my head: *Acqua passata non macina piu.* Water that's flowed past the mill grinds no more. Thinking of her causes pain to inflate inside the hollow of my chest. Sucking in a deep breath, I turn up the radio.

The rain is beating with unrelenting force across my windscreen, but the inside of my car is warm and dry. So far. I glance up at the sagging canvas roof of my Suzuki Vitara. A small bulge has formed in the centre. I'm not surprised. The car is over fifteen years old. I really should get a new one.

My left hand settles on my belly as I drive.

I look down at the speedo and realise I'm over the speed limit. I think about pressing my foot harder against the accelerator, about letting the battered four-wheel drive take me where it wants to, about how the slippery road and speed might solve all my problems.

Gianna.

Her warm hand brushes the tops of my knuckles and I take my foot off the pedal—130 ... 100 ... 90. The warm feeling disappears.

Fleeing is my superpower. When I was fourteen, I perfected the art of escape. First, into my imagination. Then, out of the house to smoke and drink stolen booze. Escaping was always a necessity, not because I was abused, or because my parents drank—my family weren't perfect ... what family is?—I was just a rebel, pure and simple. I had this surging *need* to be free. The adrenaline of sneaking out made me feel alive.

I couldn't be more different to my big sister, who was always so ethereal and kind. An image of her unfolds in my mind. Sirena was exactly what my parents expected from a girl. She loved fairy tales, pink everything, and pretty dresses. Even as an adult, her childhood teddy bears sit on a chair in her bedroom.

'To pass down to my own children.' Her mossy green eyes light up when she talks about becoming a mum.

I'm the total opposite. The mould broke when I was conceived. I lived in jeans—or shorts in summer—with t-shirts that carried some in-your-face slogan. I didn't believe in fairy tales, still don't. They give false belief that life is all about happy-ever-afters.

Water drips onto my forehead. 'Shit.' So much for warm and dry. I pound the steering wheel. The rain hasn't let up since I passed Western Sydney.

My car shudders and shakes as I pick up speed again. This time, my mother's voice barges into my thoughts.

Why? Why can I not buy my daughter a new car? It is no good you drive in an old car. I worry about you, Gianna.

I don't want anything from her.

Her love.

Her help.

Her forgiveness.

I can't stand it. I don't deserve it.

I spot a petrol station ahead. The gauge tells me I'm low on fuel and my brain tells me I need coffee and a cigarette. I shouldn't have either. I decide to compromise.

'Sure is pissing down,' the cashier says as I approach.

'We do need it,' I say automatically, sliding a bag of chocolate bullets on the counter. 'Number two. The Suzuki.'

As she rings up the register, I blurt 'And a skim latte, please' before I can change my mind. I glance at her Caltex name badge. 'Thanks, Hazel.'

'My pleasure. Where'ya heading?' she asks, turning to fill the portafilter with grounds.

'Congo.'

'It's a ghost town in winter.'

'I know. I'm running away.' I laugh, pretending it's a joke. The sound is shrill. She's probably heard it all before.

'Drive safe,' she says, as I walk out.

I settle back in the car and punch the roof to get rid of the water before placing the cup of coffee between my thighs. The heat penetrates my jeans and makes me think of his touch. Shaking off the memory, I slide an Adele CD into the player and pull out onto the road.

By the third track on the CD, the rain eases, and the setting sun peeks through grey clouds. I sneak quick glances west across the highway and see a kaleidoscope of colour spill past the bruised shadow of the Budawang Range. Only an hour to go.

On the passenger seat, my phone starts playing Blondie's 'Call Me'. Mum. I ignore it. Voice mail beeps. I wait. The phone rings again. *Whoot, there it is*, I think, giving myself a mental hi-five. Like clockwork.

'I call a second time in case you're busy and don't make it to the phone in time,' she once told me.

I know she worries. She's already lost one daughter. But she doesn't know that I disappeared the day my sister did.

I drive in silence, focusing on Adele's soulful lyrics. Her songs are the only ones I can listen to. Sirena and I were different in so many ways, but we always loved the same music. She was my concert plus one and I was always hers. Even after she got married. I smile at the memory of the Christmas when I gifted her Adele tickets.

'You didn't!' Sirena screamed as she tore open the gawdy paper.

'I did.' I beamed.

Sirena flew in my arms. 'I'll wear a nice dress. And I can help pick something out for you too?'

'No way!' I laughed and shook my head. But I knew I'd let her choose something. It would make her so happy.

I'm startled by the tune of Blondie's 'Call Me' blaring from my phone once again. I reach across and press end call. I feel cruel.

The phone rings again.

'Jesus!'

I pick it up to turn it off and see that it's Alex. For a moment, I contemplate answering, but all the sharp words and tears of our fight rush back and I throw the phone into my bag.

The tears well, and I swallow hard to contain them. In that moment, the rain returns. I huff. Maybe I should cry more. Maybe I should wail and mourn.

Maybe I should scream.

I do.

I scream.

My outburst blends with the rain on the canvas roof. And then my tear ducts betray me. I cry, hard and loud. Part of my tyre hits the grassy strip at the side of the road. I don't expect it and my hands leave the steering wheel.

The car slides and bumps out of control.

Adrenaline kicks in; I grab the wheel and press down hard on the brake. The Suzuki bucks, then fishtails, before stalling to an abrupt stop. My heart slams against my chest and I take in heavy gulps of air. A wave of nausea presses down on me. My hands shake as I unbuckle the belt and pull up the lever so the seat falls back. I lie down.

I'm so exhausted.

I stare at the raindrops bursting on the windscreen, and the watery movement calms my breathing. Disjointed memories of summer holidays with my sister float in and out of my mind, tangled with joy and pain.

Sirena loved the beach. Her favourite place was the rock pools. We'd sit in water warmed by the sun, holding hands and letting our toes float to the surface. The basin of rock, polished smooth by decades of pounding waves, would feel like a broad hand across my bare back.

One afternoon, she burst into the kitchen with a copy of Tennyson's poem 'The Mermaid' clutched in her salty hands.

'My name. My name means "mermaid"! Did you know that, Mum?' she said excitedly.

The eternal pragmatist, my mother told her that Sirena was a family name. Our family was from a seaside town in Sicily; names about the ocean and water were popular. Nonna's name, Marilla, meant 'shiny sea'. Sirena ignored this and slumped across the bench, her hand on her cheek, beaming. The mundane never spoilt her fantasies.

From then on, while I believed in Santa Claus, Sirena believed in mermaids. When we sat in the rock pools, she'd cross her ankles and flick her legs as if they were a long, luscious tail.

'Maybe if we are very quiet, the mermaids will come and sit with us,' Sirena would whisper. Her determined hope was infectious, and I played along to make her happy. It made *me* happy.

My grandmother would click her tongue if she heard us playing like this. Cursed by her name, she would say. She had always believed that water would take her.

When Sirena married, she moved to Randwick to be close to the ocean. The Mahon Rockpool was her sanctuary. Every day, rain or shine, Sirena swam laps. On my days off I'd join her, and afterwards, we'd sit on the pool's rocky edge and listen to the ocean, talking and drinking coffee from a flask. I loved those quiet moments.

Sirena was open and kind. I was nasty and stained. She married and loved with honesty. I pushed good men away. Sirena was pure goodness. I opened my body to vacant hearts and brutal hands.

Sirena was a romantic; she never gave up on me. Instead, she brought her colleague Alex home for dinner one night. I resisted, but Sirena never gave in.

When Sirena announced her pregnancy the world shone. The life growing inside her somehow made my life shine brighter as her belly swelled. Watching my sister grow with life gave me hope. Feeling the force inside as it pushed against my hand was more powerful than I imagined. The new promise of being someone's auntie softened me.

My darkness faded and I let Alex in. It wasn't perfect but it was electric. If we weren't making love, we were hurling hurtful words at each other.

The shriek of a semi-trailer's air brakes jolts me out of my fog. I open my eyes to see that dusk has settled around me. The rain has stopped. I set the seat upright and, with care, drive the Suzuki back onto the slick bitumen.

I drive through the sleepy hamlet of Moruya. I let the familiarity of the road carry me onwards, all the way into the driveway of our holiday home, where I finally unfold myself from the seat and stretch. The sound of the waves echoes across the empty sand dunes.

As I walk towards the beach, I hear our childish voices, trapped forever in the whistling wind. I follow my memory to the edge of the dune and slip off my sneakers. The wet sand sends a shiver up my spine and I see her.

She's naked, standing waist-deep in the break. Her long, dark hair cascades over her engorged breasts, and she's holding the baby who died fighting its way out of her as she lay in the shallow plastic pool in her living room.

The water had bled around her. Luke called an ambulance. She'd held my hand, her eyes filled with hope. Holding back tears, I coached her through each contraction, listening for the sirens with a silent and desperate heart.

Her hope betrayed her.

I sit on the beach and watch my sister exist where she has always wanted to be.

As dusk spills into twilight, she fades. And I feel the flutter inside my belly.

THE PROMISE

Dear Tristan,

I thought I would pop by and share some news.

The place looks tidy. The scent of those lavender and rosemary bushes brings back wonderful memories. Remember when you discovered how much I loved them when we were rehearsing *The Glass Menagerie* for our senior production? We used them as jonquils for the gentle-man-caller scene. The stage manager had forgotten the flow-ers, and you rushed outside to steal some from the church's garden next door. You came back proclaiming rosemary would help me remember my lines. I lobbed back, 'And lavender will calm *you* down.' It was the first time we actu-ally had a laugh. Your temper was epic—catastrophic compared to my incessant line mistakes.

You wore your seriousness as an impenetrable shield; the dark, brooding actor with the brilliant mind. Next to you, I felt like the ditzy brunette. I'd listen to your heated discussions with the director—what was his name? Gary? Graham? ... Tony! That's it!

It's funny how we forget the inconsequential things. Do

you like my choice of word, 'inconsequential'? You taught me to admire words. I now relish unique and poetic ones. I think of them like Lindt balls: hard at first, taking up a lot of room in your mouth, but then the chocolate melts, coating your tongue.

I hope you don't mind, but I helped myself to—well, stolen—some lavender and rosemary to place under my pillow. Now it's time for my audition. I don't want to jinx it by telling you any details. Yet. I'll let you know how I go.

All my love,
Isabel

DEAR TRISTAN,

I've dropped by to share some news. This is so exciting. I've been preparing for ... drum roll, please ... a *callback!* Can you believe it? Of course you can. You always believed in me. I need to prepare two monologues: a contemporary and a classic piece. I'm definitely doing Maggie's scene from *Cat on a Hot Tin Roof* for the contemporary. And I *was* thinking of Lady Macbeth's 'unsex me' scene, but everyone does that one. I don't know which one of The Bard's monologues would suit me. You would know.

I've been reciting my lines among your rosemary and lavender, which, by the way, are thriving, their leaves weeping from the morning rain. The bushes are an obedient audience, listening to this Australian girl butcher Maggie's Texan accent.

The old lady next door is weeding her marigolds and, by the look on her face, thinks I'm bonkers, but I don't care.

Maybe I *am* nuts. Like Maggie, I'm lonely. Knowing that you can't love me back makes me sad. Look, I know you don't like displays of sentimentality, but ... those stars that come out each night. Well, they're all pieces of my shattered heart.

I've done it now. Swollen tears are tumbling, and the lady next door looks like she's going to come over and give me a hug. I should go.

All my love,

Isabel

DEAR TRISTAN,

I just had to come by and tell you ... I got it! I got the part. My celebrity signature, all practised in looping curves, is going to sing across my contract.

I'm getting used to you not being here. Is that sad?

I've missed sitting here in the fresh air, writing under the shade of the flame tree. Its fevered red petals brush against the cerulean sky, reminiscent of a Gauguin painting. Did you see what I did? My description for blue? I can't take all the credit.

I was feeling a little low yesterday, waiting for my agent to call. To pass the time, I watched *The Devil Wears Prada*. The last movie we saw together. I'm so grateful for Meryl Streep. The only reason you agreed to watch it with me was your admiration for her. I know you'll never admit it, but I saw it—subtle, yes, but it was there: a tiny tear hidden in your lashes before you brushed it away. I wanted to kiss you. I wish I had.

I think a lot about that promise you made last summer. Do you remember? Dare I say it? Does it matter now?

The storm hit just as rehearsals finished, and we sheltered under the awning. It was our second production together. The company loved our chemistry as Laura and Tom, and they'd approached us to play Elizabeth Bennett and Mr Darcy in a new adaption of *Pride and Prejudice*. The rain was teeming down. We'd had hours of being on our feet and we were both shattered, so I shared my chicken and avocado sandwich with you. I'd smothered it with my special concoction of mayonnaise and wasabi, and I beamed when you said I was an excellent cook. Then you held my hand and looked at me intently, your brown eyes blazing, little creases sketched above the bridge of your nose. You promised that if we weren't married by thirty, we'd marry each other. I thought you were joking, which is why I laughed. But you stood silent, taking in deep, languid breaths.

That's when I fell in love with you.

I remember how our director, Kate, vetoed any lip action in rehearsals, directing us not to kiss until opening night, to contain any passionate energy and recreate the fragile moment of a first kiss. I'll never forget when you, as Mr Darcy, finally kissed me, as Elizabeth. I felt every sensual part of me awaken. A charged stillness filled the auditorium. Soft weeping floated through the air like dust caught in a spotlight. 'Such talented actors,' everyone thought.

I think you knew I wasn't acting.

All my love,

Isabel

DEAR TRISTAN,

I know it's been months since my last visit. I finished filming yesterday, and the movie comes out next year. How strange it will be to see my face looming across the silver screen.

I don't know how to say this. I wish I could tell you in person, to see your smile—slight at first before expanding with pride.

... They've cast me in a play. In London. It's Patrick Marber's *Closer*. I got the role of Alice! It's my big break.

So I'm moving away. I can't keep pining for you.

Tristan, I owe you so much for your belief in me, not just as an actor, but as a person who had something to offer—emotionally and intellectually. We've come such a long way since drama class and acting school. After each rejection, you picked me up and encouraged me to try again, making sure I kept auditioning year after year. Your support and advice meant the world.

Next week, I turn thirty. I'm not married, and unless someone jumps out of the flame tree and proposes to me, I'll still be single. Who would've thought a man like you, a man of his word, would renege on his promise?

Maybe I'll fall in love with my leading man and you'll be off the hook. Legitimately. (I'm joking. There's a broad grin slathered across my face.)

Now don't cringe. I know how much you hate it when I quote movie lines, but ...

Hang on, I need some tissues.

Okay, here goes.

I'm just a girl, standing in front of a boy, asking him to love her.

Are you cursing Julia Roberts and *Notting Hill*?

Tristan, this is a temporary goodbye. I will see you again. You ~~have~~ will always matter to me.

Look after these southern stars for me. They shine down for you.

All my love,
Isabel

DEAR MS MOORE,

Due to ground instability at the cemetery, the council has instructed us to move the permanent urns in the northern sector. While we were moving Tristan Boyd's ashes, we discovered these letters in a porcelain box. We weren't at liberty to open them, but we contacted the next of kin and received your address from Gina Boyd. We understand the sentimentality regarding mementos left for loved ones who have departed, and are mindful that these remembrances don't get damaged or lost.

Miss Boyd believes that these letters will be safe with you until we've completed the relocation. Unfortunately, we are unable to store them at the church, due to extensive restorations and renovations underway.

Please find enclosed the letters and the porcelain box.

We paid for all postage as a courtesy for the inconvenience caused.

Yours sincerely,
Fr Robert Morton
Parish Priest
Saint Anthony of Padua

DEAR ISABEL,

I never realised that you left letters for Tristan. I'm ashamed. I could never go to the cemetery. I'm so glad you did. It was too painful for me, a reminder that my big brother would no longer be around to tease me and make me feel safe. His suicide gouged a hole in all our hearts. My only consolation has been knowing that he's with Mum and Dad. I don't think he ever forgave himself for being the one driving the car that night. Losing them was difficult for me, but it took the light out of Tristan's life.

Maybe that wasn't the only reason. Do we ever know what's going on in people's minds?

One thing I'm certain of is that he adored you. He spoke about you all the time. He loved you.

I've been following your career. You're doing so well. Tristan would be proud.

All my love,

Gina

THE PHOTO

'Are you sure this is where you want to be dropped off, love?'

'Yep. I grew up here.' Ruby held out her hand as the driver passed over her change.

He still looked curious. The same way he had when she'd hailed him. She couldn't blame him. It was nearly midnight, and the place was deserted—a ghost town in winter. Even in summer, Norah Head would close for the night at 9 p.m.

'Here, take this.' The cabbie gave Ruby a business card. 'Call if you need to.'

When she'd gotten off the train from Sydney, she'd waited nearly forty minutes for a bus that never came. In her desperation to get to the holiday house, she'd started walking, knowing it would take her over an hour to get there on foot. The taxi driver, who was on his way home, had stopped.

A father with daughters of his own, he'd been quite vocal about her being out alone at night. She put up with the lecture—being inside the warm taxi was worth it.

Ruby stood on the footpath and shivered as the taxi drove away. She zipped her hoodie up tight. Unease washed over her as she surveyed the hushed cul-de-sac. All the houses were in shadow, packed up and in hibernation for the winter months. It was quiet, eerie.

The briny air reminded her how close they were to the cliff. The ocean surged far below them at the end of the road, as if the construction crew had planned to continue but gave up when they discovered the water that lay in their path. Towards the east, she could just make out the tips of fluorescent waves and hear the ocean pounding the headland. It was like a faint roar as each one crashed upon the sandstone cliff face and rocks. The lighthouse, which was directly out to sea from the cul-de-sac, beamed its artificial light, panning across the watery landscape. With each cycle, the street before her lit up before falling into darkness again.

Ruby's hair whipped her face. She slipped the elastic off her wrist and pulled her hair into a messy bun. Then, shoving her hands deep inside the pockets of her hoodie, she crossed the road. A lone streetlight in the dead-end cul-de-sac provided a flickering glow to add to the lighthouse beam.

The sight of her family's modest summer home filled Ruby with sadness. It held memories of youthful adventures and innocent joy, of summer days filled with backyard cricket, beach trips, and board games. This seaside cottage, once the centre of a happy family, now stood abandoned.

She blamed her father. For whatever reason, he stopped loving her mum. Stopped being kind. Stopped showing his wife any affection. Instead treating her like she was a burden in his life. Refusing to believe the relationship was over, she'd gripped tight to the crumbling marriage for nearly five years. And the tighter she held, the nastier he became. Infidelity was the final cruel blow that shattered their marriage. Her father packed up and left. His departure left a dark void for her mother, but brought relief and emotional respite to Ruby.

Over those years, she watched her mum's boundless joy wither, watched her become withdrawn. When her father left, Ruby dropped by as often as her university and work schedule allowed, but the constant worry about her mum's state took its toll. It wasn't always easy to visit her.

Her mum got the family house in the divorce. Her father remained emotionally cold, but Ruby knew he didn't want to leave her mum destitute. A year after Ruby started her bachelor's in design computing, a room became available on campus and she moved there. A few months later, her mum sold the family home and downsized to a cottage in Lawson in the Blue Mountains. This helped her financially, freeing up the assets to help her make ends meet.

With her mum over an hour from campus, visiting became more difficult. This worried her. Over the last eighteen months, the sadness her mother carried grew stronger. In their weekly video calls, Ruby had started to notice more and more her mother's sunken eyes. There was a gauntness in them that stared back at her through the screen and made her stomach twist.

A few weeks ago, she'd tried to talk to her brother about it.

'I think she's depressed. She's fading away to nothing.'

'Let it go,' Gino had thrown back.

But she couldn't. A deep-rooted anxiety had settled inside her. Something wasn't right.

The previous week, Ruby had gone to her mother's

house in the afternoon to find it empty. By twilight, her mother still hadn't returned.

In a panic, she'd called Gino for a second time.

'Stop pandering to her.'

'I'm not. I'm worried. Why aren't you?'

'You know what she's like. Always so bloody dramatic. It's tiring.'

Ruby slammed the phone down. 'Fucking arsehole.' She hated Gino for his lack of empathy and compassion.

There was no way she was giving up on a woman who'd committed herself to her family. Yes, her mother loved with intensity, and that could sometimes be all-consuming for those around her, but she was in pain. How could she turn away?

For days after that, Ruby had trouble concentrating, despite the quiet of the dorm. Everyone was locked away in their rooms, studying for the upcoming exams. She worried so much about her mum that she was distracted in lectures and missed significant prep notes for her final assignment.

That evening in her dorm room, she'd called her mum again. No answer. Her chest tightened. *Where are you?* She needed chocolate. As she reached up for her stash on the bookshelf, her cardigan sleeve caught the side of a photo frame. The glass cracked when it landed on her desk. Ruby shook her head. Nothing was ever simple anymore.

But something made her pick up the frame. It held her favourite photo, taken the summer before she began high school. That had been the last summer they'd spent as a happy family. Before the years of pain, before her father met Sarina. She pulled the picture out of the shattered glass.

That's when the revelation had seized her—the cottage at Norah Head. That's where her mum had to be. That place held powerful memories. It was a connection to the time when they'd all been together.

She'd shoved the photo in her bag and sprinted out the door to get to Central Station and catch the late train up the coast.

Now, walking up the path to the house, anxiety engulfed her. No lights were on. What if her mum wasn't here? Ruby scanned the windows and then spotted it—a flickering light. The television.

She's here!

Her mother always fell asleep in front of the TV.

She placed her palm on the front door. The paint flaked off under her touch, the result of years of salt spray. Ruby fumbled at the lock, but the door was already ajar. Her pulse kicked up a notch. She pushed it open, its hinges crying out in protest, and crept in. The house was silent, the air stagnant. The stale, musty smell was familiar—it was the smell that always greeted them on the first visit back to the cottage after it had been shut up for winter. Her mum clearly hadn't been here long.

Ruby walked down the hallway and spotted her mum's black handbag on the wall hook.

'Hello?' She crept into the lounge and turned off the soundless TV. 'Mum?' Ruby paused and cocked her ear.

Her panic escalating, she flicked the switch for the kitchen light. Nothing happened. She toggled the switch to see if she could spark it to life. Still nothing. Ruby held her breath and listened, allowing her eyes to adjust to the dark and waiting for the lighthouse beam to appear and interrupt the blackness.

Bang!

She jumped, but realised it was the wooden screen door

hammering against the door frame. As she rushed forward to secure it in place, she spotted her.

'Mum!'

Her mum was slumped against the veranda wall, her eyes closed. There was an unlit candle next to her and family albums scattered all around. One of them was open on her lap, its pages riddled with gaping empty squares where the photos were missing.

Her mum didn't respond.

Ruby fumbled for her phone and rang triple zero as the tears that had been building erupted out of her.

On the floor lay a photo of her lost brother.

'*PADRE NOSTRO, Ave Maria, Gloria al Padre, Sacro Cuore di Gesù, ripongo tutta la mia fiducia in te.*'

Ruby stirred. The humming of repeated words was interlaced with a jumble of beeps. She forced her eyes open. A spasm constricted her neck when she lifted her head off her folded arms. Dazed and groggy, she worked to establish her bearings.

Her focus sharpened.

Cocooned in a sterile hospital blanket lay her mother. Tubes ran in and out of her body. Ruby stretched. The chair creaked and groaned under her weight.

The mild scent of rosemary mingled with the stronger smell of antiseptic.

'*Mi cara*, Rubina.' A voice floated in.

Ruby found herself being yanked up and held tight against a soft bosom. She took in the scent of talcum powder and lemon verbena. *Nonna*. A calmness descended on her.

The hug took her back to a time when she was ten. Her

nonna had soothed her after she'd gotten into a scrape trying to keep up with her older brothers.

A militant nurse disturbed their tender moment. 'Visiting hours are over.' She marched in and snapped the curtain abruptly, hiding Ruby's unconscious mother.

'I think we are not welcome.' Nonna glared at the closed screen.

The nurse whisked the curtain open. 'Pardon?'

Waving the nurse's question away, Nonna muttered, '*Disgraziata.*' Then she took Ruby's hand. '*Andiamo. Vuoi un caffè?*'

Ruby nodded. She was desperate for a strong cup of coffee.

So that she could adjust herself on her walking stick, Nonna handed the jar of water and little bale of rosemary she was holding to Ruby.

'What were you saying when I woke up?'

'A prayer for your mamma.' She passed Ruby a little card with the Virgin Mary on the front.

Ruby turned it over.

OUR FATHER
Hail Mary
Glory be to the Father
Sacred Heart of Jesus,
I place all my trust in you.

JUST READING the words calmed her. Ruby glanced up. '*Grazie*, Nonna.'

Nonna waved away her thanks and signalled for Ruby to hand back the water and rosemary. 'It is holy water.'

Of course. This was what Nonna always did in times of joy, change, and sadness. A devout Catholic who spent her days worrying about her grandchildren—especially after they stopped attending Mass once their interest in the opposite sex blossomed—Nonna had made it her spiritual mission to keep her family in the good grace of God.

Once they'd settled in the hospital café, Ruby took a moment to decompress. It was early. Just before 7 a.m. Only a few people sat on the white plastic tables and chairs. A group of bleary-eyed interns huddled together, talking in hushed tones. A woman, whose head was wrapped in a blue scarf dotted with clouds, consoled the man she was with. Maybe her husband. His head hung low to hide his tears. She was connected to a machine at her side that beeped, breaking the silence at regular intervals, the sound a reminder of where they were. Ruby's heart lurched at the sight of the tubes sprouting out of her dressing gown, but the woman's attempt to colour coordinate lifted Ruby's spirits a little.

Nonna squeezed Ruby's arm. Ruby placed her hand on top and smiled. She was grateful her grandmother was with her.

'How did you get here?' Nonna had never learned to drive.

'I woke Zio Marco after you called. The kind ambulance lady helped me gather information. You were very upset.'

Ruby cringed. While the paramedics had attended to her mother, she'd called Nonna in hysterics. The ambulance officer had needed to take the phone from Ruby and speak to her nonna for her.

'I'm sorry I upset you.'

'Is okay. The lady was kind. She told me you were in

shock.' She placed her hand on Ruby's cheek. 'You are okay now.'

Ruby nodded jerkily. 'Where's Zio now?'

'Calling Gino.'

'As if he'd worry.' Ruby slumped back in her chair. It squealed against the tiles. A couple of nearby patrons glanced in her direction. 'Gino doesn't care, and we haven't heard from Peter in years.'

Her grandmother sighed. 'Your mother has been speaking with Peter.'

'What? When?' Ruby leaned hard across the table, irritation flaring in her gut. Her brothers' actions and attitudes only fed her family's dysfunction. During her brothers' broody and turbulent teenage years, her relationship with them broke down. They were never interested in spending any time with her.

'They are becoming men,' her mother had lamented.

Without a positive male role model, they ran wild. Gino always blamed his mum for their dad leaving and carried an arrogant anger that hurt her mother. Peter was lost. Always looking for a way to escape their mother's debilitating sadness.

Not only had her mother lost her husband to infidelity, but over the years she also lost the respect and attention of her sons. Even when she was young, Ruby had been annoyed with how much maternal energy her mum invested in her brothers, who didn't seem to notice.

Ruby caught Nonna calmly scrutinising her with a look reserved almost exclusively for perceptive therapists; a look Ruby recognised because she'd seen her fair share of them.

'Why didn't Mum tell us? Tell *me*?'

'Rubina. Your mamma did not want you to worry.'

'Well, it's a bit late for that.' Ruby folded her arms

across her chest. She opened her mouth again, but Nonna reached out and placed her index finger in the centre of her lips and shushed her.

'I will tell you.'

'Tell me what?'

'About Peter.'

'You know where he is?' The hurt of being kept in the dark hit Ruby at her core. 'Why didn't anybody tell me?! You all know how much I've missed him. How much I've worried about him.' Hot tears stung her eyes.

'Because he didn't want anyone to know. Your mother promised him.'

'But *you* knew.'

'I am his grandmother.'

'And I'm his *sister*.' Ruby knew she was being rude, but she didn't care. 'Well? Where is he?!'

Peter had always been the adventurous one. Never able to sit still for long, he'd always been the sibling that would get himself into mischief—falling out of trees, stacking his bike, skipping classes. He hated school and was constantly compared to Gino and Ruby, who were studious and talented. As soon as he turned sixteen, he abandoned his education and got a job working as a gardener for rich urbanites who owned five-acre blocks on the outskirts of Sydney.

Then one day, the divorce still a festering wound for the family, he left. No warning. No note. Nothing.

Her brother's departure had broken her mother's heart. Her father was preoccupied with his new family, the new baby on the way. He channelled all fatherly concern into them and forgot about his old life, his other children. When he found out about Peter's disappearance, he shrugged and said they couldn't do any more for him.

'So, where is he now?' A sudden thought slapped her. 'Shit! Drugs! Is he in trouble? Oh my God.'

After the divorce, Peter experimented with drugs. At sixteen, he'd been picked up by the cops when they saw him rolling a joint in their local park. Unlike Ruby, who hated her father for what he did, Peter missed him.

Ruby worried he still turned to drugs for solace. He wasn't like Ruby or Gino. He'd never been able to push through the shitty parts of life. He felt every pain, keenly.

'Nonna, tell me!' Her shrill voice pierced the hushed murmurings of the café, and several more people glanced her way.

'*Silenzio*,' her nonna hissed with authority. Despite being four-foot-nothing and walking with a shuffle, she commanded more attention than a school principal. 'Stop with the loud words.'

'Sorry,' Ruby said quickly. She picked up her coffee and took a sip to evade her grandmother's annoyed gaze. Ruby placed the cup back on the saucer and concentrated on it, trying to suppress the tears building in her throat.

'Yes, Peter is on the drugs, Rubina. He is not well.'

'What?' A coldness surged through her veins. 'I need to know. What's going on?' Her words came out sharp and clipped.

'You must calm down, Rubina. It is no good for you to be like this.' Her nonna reached over the table and clutched her hand. 'It is not like you think. He is on the drugs, but not the bad ones.' With shaky hands, she opened her purse and took out a white handkerchief. Ruby watched the finely embroidered flowers ripple and fold as her grandmother dabbed at her eyes.

A niggling feeling of shame tugged at her heart. Ruby swallowed the lump in her throat. 'Nonna?' She spoke more gently this time. 'Where is Peter? Does Gino know Mum's been talking to him? Do they both know about Mum's stroke?'

'*Si.*'

Ruby tapped the table. Annoyance swelled inside her. 'And Peter? Where is he now? Can I see him? Where has been all these years?' She needed all the details. Quickly.

'He is gone.'

'Again?' Why was Peter doing this to her, to their family? She dropped her head onto her hands.

'Peter is different, Rubina. *Una pecora nero.*'

'He's not a black sheep, Nonna. I hate that term. It makes him sound bad. He's not bad. He's just different. We should've embraced that.' The tears threatened to come again. 'Where did it all go wrong? Why can't we just go back to being the happy clan we used to be? Before ...' She sniffed.

'Before?'

Ruby snatched her backpack from the floor and rummaged inside until she found the photo—the catalyst for sending her up the coast to their holiday home. 'This was the last time we were a happy family.'

It was all too much. Her mum's mini stroke. Finding out that Peter had returned, only to leave again. To have him confirm through his actions that, even after all this time, he still didn't want to see her.

RUBY WHEELED her mum through the hospital grounds. Nonna pounded the ground with her walking stick. It was an unusually warm August morning, and Ruby's mum had expressed a desire to get out in the fresh air. To enjoy the vibrant flowers. She missed her garden back in Lawson.

Ten days had passed since her stroke and if all the tests came back positive, she could go home in a couple of days. Her mum was recovering quickly, with no permanent damage. The mini stroke had been a warning. The hospital's physiotherapist and dietician had been working with her on ways to change her lifestyle, encouraging her to exercise and reduce her stress. Her mum had also made the brave decision to connect with the resident psychologist. Ruby noticed a new aura of contentment surrounding her.

She parked the wheelchair next to a bench directly in front of a sea of colour: geraniums, impatiens, wallflowers. A soft breeze accentuated the sweet fragrances.

Once her mum and grandmother were comfortable, Ruby sat down on the grass at their feet. She let the sun caress her face. Her mum and Nonna bantered in Italian, lobbing their responses with animated hand gestures. It was comforting to hear the warmth and adoration they had for each other. For the first time in years, bliss embraced her whole being. She understood the vast affection that spanned three generations—grandmother, mother, and daughter. It was this secure, unconditional love that had allowed them to sustain a resilient connection through all the heartache of the past few years.

No one had mentioned Peter recently, as all the focus had been on her mum's recovery. Even though she was desperate to see him, Ruby didn't want to upset her mother by asking lots of questions. Peter was stubborn. He lived on adrenaline and adventure. He had always ignored the potential severity of the consequences of his actions and had been swift to cast away crucial advice.

'Ruby?' Her mum stroked her hair.

Ruby lifted herself onto her knees, and her mum smiled, reached down, and touched her cheek. She'd missed that smile so much. 'Nonna told me about the photo.'

'Photo?'

'Yes, the one of all of us before your father left. I always wondered where it got to. I thought Peter had taken it.'

'Peter?' Ruby frowned. 'No, I took it when I left for uni. Sorry. I should've asked.' Ruby glanced at her nonna, then her mother. Maybe the time was right. She took a deep breath. 'What's going on with Peter, Mum? Really?'

Her mother gathered up Ruby's hands and guided her onto the bench. 'Peter broke into the holiday house a few months ago when he needed a place to stay. He discovered the photo albums. I found them scattered around the living room when I arrived, and several were missing. I thought we'd been robbed, but nothing else was taken. I knew it must have been Peter.'

'Why didn't you tell me?'

'I didn't want to make you sad. I know how much you miss him.'

'We all do. Well, not Gino.'

'Rubina!' Nonna said sternly. 'He is still your brother.'

'Sorry.'

'Gino carries his hurt in his own way.' Her mum placed a loose strand of hair back around Ruby's ear. 'Be kind to him. Anyway, Peter came to see me shortly after that and said he'd spent all night looking at them. He told me the pictures gave him hope.'

'Hope? Why?'

'Tell her,' Nonna said to her mother, as they exchanged a glance.

'You know, Peter is not well.' She placed her hand on

Ruby's cheek. Her mother's face held a calmness she hadn't seen in a long time.

HE'D TURNED up at her mother's house a few months earlier. At first, she didn't recognise her son. When she hugged him, she felt his bones protruding sharply underneath his t-shirt. Her once healthy middle child had faded away. Not wanting to spook him and cause him to flee, she maintained a discreet emotional distance and did what any Italian mother would do—she invited him in and cooked for him.

Peter ate in silence. Afterwards, he went to bed in his old room.

She spent the entire night checking on him, refusing to allow herself to go to sleep. His gauntness terrified her. Call it mother's intuition, but she sensed something grave had taken hold of her son.

The next morning, Peter found her in the backyard.

'The garden looks great, Mum.'

She focused on the spray of water.

'Mum?' Peter moved close and reached for her free hand.

Unable to hold back the tears any longer, she clutched her son and sobbed. '*Mio caro*. My dear boy. What has happened?'

'Why don't we have some coffee and I'll tell you about it.'

Settled at the kitchen table, she reached over and touched his tattooed arm. 'These are interesting. Where did you get them?

'All over.'

Peter turned his arm. On the inside was an image of a lighthouse. The beam drawn like a halo. Waves crashed at its base. It had a Japanese woodcut feel to it. His mother ran her fingers and traced the curves. She discovered a mermaid coming out of the water and sitting on the rocks at the base.

Peter placed his hand over his mother's. 'This one is my connection to home. To a happier time.'

'Summers. Before your father—' she stopped. She didn't want to tarnish this quiet moment with her son.

'I know, Mum.'

He gave her a smile and her heart swelled. She missed that smile.

'Peter, where have you been?'

He shared stories about his time fruit picking in southern NSW and working long hours as a farmhand in Victoria. About hitchhiking north to New Italy to find work on a dairy farm and finally finding a job in Southeast Queensland as a labourer.

He was interrupted by a coughing fit that paralysed and shook his weakened body. She got up and filled a glass with tap water.

She watched him carefully as he reached for a silver sleeve of pills and pushed four yellow tablets out through the foil. Peter held them in his palm and stared at them. Then, taking the glass from her, he threw the tablets into his mouth and washed them down.

'Tell me the truth. Are you okay?' She waited.

This time, Peter reached across the kitchen table. The youthful hands his mother remembered were now worn and aged. She welcomed the touch of his cool, callused skin.

He searched her face. 'I'm sick. Very sick.'

'WHAT'S WRONG WITH HIM?' Ruby had listened to her mother's story with ever-increasing anxiety. Even though she was beginning to have her suspicions, she had to hear it from her mum's lips.

'Cancer.'

The word sliced a gash in Ruby's chest. She closed her eyes. 'What kind?'

'Throat. The drinking, the drugs—he was never well. Yes, he ran away. But not from us. From himself.'

'But why stay away now? We can help him!' Ruby faced her mother and looked at her pleadingly, desperate for an answer. Something to help her make sense of all of this.

Her mum held her hand. 'He is not the same. But I know he still cares.'

'*Gli e' mancato la sua famiglia,*' Nonna offered.

Her mum smiled. '*Si,* Nonna is right. Peter may be lost, but deep down he knows he's still a part of this family.'

Ruby stood. 'Does he?' Her voice cracked. 'We're all grieving. We have been for years, all of us, but in secret. We've all been too scared to share our feelings!'

Her mum reached up and touched her arm. 'I know this is hard.'

Ruby crumpled into her mum's embrace, completely drained. She wiped away the tears meandering down her cheeks.

Nonna tucked a handkerchief into her hand. Once her tears petered to a stop, Ruby blew her nose. 'Will Peter ever come home?'

There was a pause. Nonna's faith broke the silence. '*Chi si volta, e chi si gira, sempre a casa va finire.*'

Her mother nodded. 'No matter where you turn, you'll always end up at home.'

The old Italian saying gave Ruby some hope. There

wasn't much she could control, she understood that now. Her family wasn't perfect, but then again, whose family was? As she sat, flanked by her grandmother and mum, two women who'd endured pain in their own ways, she knew she was blessed. Their love would never end. She understood.

We all end up back home eventually. Ruby smiled. Love would be their beacon.

THE DISCOVERY

The siren faded. The clickity-clack of the city train rumbled under the open window, while Friday night revellers whistled and shouted as they returned home, full of booze and cigarettes.

Leena stirred. What the heck was that rustling? Drowsy, she reached down towards the floor for Dixie and found nothing. Where was the cat?

Her ankle slammed into the side of the sofa as she stretched. Annoyed, she kicked the couch then smacked her lips together in an attempt to alleviate the dryness that layered her tongue like a worn Persian rug. Dank and stiff.

She shivered and pulled her dressing gown tighter around her body. The threadbare couch was the only place she could drift off. Her bedroom reminded her of a concrete mausoleum.

And now the frenetic rustling.

She eased herself up and noticed the takeaway bag on the coffee table in front of her. Leena sniffed at the half-eaten burger inside and gagged. She shuffled to the kitchen and discarded the cold dinner in the bin.

She filled a glass with tap water. It ran cold down her throat and soothed the dryness in her mouth. Outside, the belly of the night settled around her as drunken strangers rounded the corner and faded into the dark. She took another sip of water and glanced at the oven clock. Nearly 4 a.m.

The rustling sounded again, a dull echo against the damp, stained walls. Leena remembered the box at the end of the hallway.

Silly cat. She's trapped herself inside.

But the box was empty.

More rustling. It was coming from the spare room. *That's all I need. Mice.*

Leena flipped on the light and couldn't help but chuckle. 'Whatcha got there, little lady?'

Dixie lay long on the floor in the spare bedroom, scratching at a bundle of papers fanned out and scattered away from an upturned gift box. The room was permeated with the unpleasant odour of mothballs. Boxes of shoes, crates packed with china and ornaments, and garbage bags bursting with her mother's clothes littered the space. All vintage, yet sentimental. Memories shoved out of sight, waiting for Leena to decide what to do with them.

After the funeral, Leena had spent a couple of week-ends separating the sentimental pieces from items destined for the Salvos.

It didn't take long. Most of the items were already boxed and in storage. A month before she died, her mum became quite insistent to get her belongings sorted.

'Always organised and prepared, aren't you, Mum?' Leena forced a smile as she placed a cup of tea down in front of her, followed by a glass filled with ice cubes to help with the nausea. She'd come down from Sydney for a few days and help her mum with daily tasks. This round of chemotherapy was proving to be more brutal than the last.

'Well, I'm terminal. Someone's got to do it.'

The comment tore at Leena's heart. She fell silent, the words lodged in her throat. Tears threatened to fall as her mum placed her hand onto Leena's.

'Why wait until I'm gone.' Her tired eyes offered warmth and love. 'This way I can tell you what's worth keeping and what can go to a new home.'

Leena couldn't argue with her; her mum would help no matter what, even on the days the treatment weakened and tired her quickly. Instead, Leena smiled and went along with it.

During the cleanout, Leena came across her mother's will. 'Are you sure about this clause? I don't think there'll be a lot of buyers who'd be willing to wait until you die to settle.' A surge of emotion pushed the air out of her lungs. She caught her breath, her eyes filling with tears. 'It's so morbid, Mum.'

Her mum reached across and patted Leena's cheek. 'It is better if they settle after I die, no?'

Leena squeezed her mum's hand and nodded. She was right. It was her house and she deserved to know she had a home right to the end.

Leena hadn't been surprised that the house sold quickly. A cashed-up Sydneysider had snatched the 1960s beach-front bungalow. Owning property with uninterrupted ocean views, only a couple of hours drive south from Sydney, was a desirable investment.

Her mother's death had sharpened Leena's alienation. There had been friends over the years, but all of them were gone now, moved overseas or interstate with new husbands or careers. Promises of 'We'll keep in touch' had been bandied about to soften the use-by dates of their friend-ships. With her mother's treatments and care, she found it hard to commit to social events. Guilt pressed down on her constantly. Knowing her mum was alone on the south coast, dealing with the treatment on her own. She took on over-time to make up for hours lost when she needed to be with her mum, which ate away what was left of her social life. People had called to ask her out, but over time the calls ceased.

Leena teased the crumpled and torn paper from under Dixie's paw. 'You're a cheeky little bugger, aren't you?'

She flicked the papers at Dixie and enticed her to swat back. Then she lifted a bundle of cards wrapped in an old school ribbon. 'You old softie.'

Packed inside the box was a collection of items Leena had never seen before, including a bundle of letters written in Italian with a slanted, delicate hand; a stack of Polaroids peeping out from under the faded paper; crumbling, dried flowers; and a book of Mary Oliver's poetry. A faint waft of perfume escaped. Her mother's scent.

Leena picked up the photos first. They were of her mother and another woman—both looked about seventeen. The other woman reminded Leena of a dark-haired Marilyn Monroe. Leena smiled at a photo of the two of them laughing on a Vespa.

She shuffled through the images. A photo of her mother sitting in the woman's lap, both reading a glossy magazine, made her pause. Leena suddenly felt intrusive.

At twenty years old, her newly married parents migrated to Sydney from a small town near Bari, Italy. He'd left when she was little, and her mother had been reluctant to share any details. Leena always wondered about her father.

'It was a sad time,' she would say, then slap away further questions with an angry retort.

Still, Leena was desperate for answers.

'We must leave our ghosts of the past buried and forgotten,' her mother had said firmly. 'There's no reason to talk about things that are over.'

But now, her curiosity newly piqued, Leena wondered if the box held clues to her mother's refusal to talk about her father or why he'd left. Buried at the bottom was a perfume bottle with a tiny crack in the lid; over the years, the liquid had seeped out and laced the contents with its delicate scent. Leena breathed it in deeply and took out more photos —faded collections of people from her mother's old life in Italy.

She opened the anthology of poetry and thumbed the pages. A photo fluttered out. Leena gasped. It was of the same woman who'd been in the other photos. She sat on a mussed-up bed, a loose bedsheet around her voluptuous body, her breast peeking out. She was laughing at the person behind the camera.

A handwritten note, in English, was scrawled across the back, in the same hand as the letters. The date: six months after Leena's birth.

Dearest Gabriela,

I think about you all the time. I know we promised that our secret would be ours to keep.

But I cannot forget your touch, your warm body. I visit our place and I feel you.

Your kisses. Your passion.

How can I forget?

Please write. If this is all I can have, then I will accept this.

With a tender and loving heart,
Marissa xxx

In shocked silence, Leena tipped the rest of the box's contents onto the floor and sifted for ... what?

There were only letters. Secrets locked inside Italian words and phrases.

The early warble of a magpie startled her. A pink dawn bled across the grey sky.

Leena reached across the bed and grabbed the photo frame on the bedside table. The photo soothed her. Her mum looking happy, healthy, and full of life. It had been taken on a road trip, two years before the cancer diagnosis. Leena smiled at the memory. She had grabbed her mum and taken it as a selfie. The surprise made her mum laugh and so the photo captured an honest and loving moment.

Leena lifted her fingers to mouth, kissed them, and placed them on the image of her mother. '*Ti amo*, mum.' Tears stung at her eyes, and she wiped them away with the bed sheet. 'Your secrets are safe with me.'

She put the items back into the box as Dixie purred against her skin. It was time for Leena to pack away her own grief, too. Her life had been consumed with caring for her mum, burying her, mourning.

It was time for her to collect new memories.

PURPLE HONEY

Come on …

I punched the traffic light button again and scanned the relentless stream of traffic as it flowed up and down the city's busiest road. I contemplated making a dash through it, but a little voice inside my mind jabbed a warning. Getting smacked by a car wasn't on the agenda for the day.

I waited. And waited. Across the road, grey and glass skyscrapers loomed above me. Car horns blasted in irritation while I jiggled on the edge of the gutter and sucked in the pungent stench of exhaust fumes and stale drains. My temples pounded as I recalled Zia Marietta's panicked voice: 'Your mother is coming.'

The rapid beep-beep-beeping of the traffic light sent me scrambling to race to the other side of the street. I clutched my handbag to my chest as a swell of grey and navy polyester tussled me across. Safe on the other side, I stopped abruptly to double-check the address on the letter. An annoyed 'tsk' sounded behind me, but I had no time to apologise.

I hurried down the street, checking the plaques on the

doors as I went. *Number 71 ... 79 ... 97. Shit.* Missed it. Why couldn't these buildings follow a logical numbering system?

I peeped at my watch, then raced along the front of the office towers looking for number 85. I muttered 'Thank Christ' as I spotted it, then sent up a pious apology for taking the Lord's name in vain.

Composing myself, I negotiated the rotating doors and emerged into a foyer resembling something one might find in a Medici manor house. A sleek Perspex desk sat in the centre of the space, so clear and polished that the computer it held appeared to be levitating. I approached the receptionist, embarrassed by the squeaking my rubber soles made on the polished marble floor. She was on the phone. My fingers tapped out a silent beat on my thigh and I checked my watch again—I was minutes away from being officially late.

Immaculate men and women wearing Armani and Dolce & Gabbana sailed by. The sterile clip of their spiked heels echoed in the vast foyer. In my cotton dress and cheap ballet flats, I felt like a fashion stain on the building. I gave the receptionist a strained smile, silently urging her to finish her call.

'*Buongiorno.* Welcome to Palazzo, Delgi, and Partners,' she finally purred in a subtle Italian accent. 'How may I help you?'

'Hello.' I cleared my throat, but my voice still cracked. 'I'm here for the reading of my father's will. Mr Gennaro Trevisani. I'm his daughter. Zara.' Tears welled in my eyes.

Her face softening, she lifted a box of tissues from the desk and offered it to me and I plucked a couple of sheets out. Her gold bangles chimed a public announcement of my grief. 'I am sorry for your loss.' With a manicured hand, she directed my gaze. 'Please take the elevator to level ten.'

I gave her a watery smile in thanks and dashed to catch the lift. My anxiety climbed with the elevator. *Deep breaths. In ... out ... in ... out ...*

I wiped my sweaty palms against the sides of my dress.

Please, God, please keep her away today—just for today. Bracing myself for an unanswered prayer, I exited the elevator and followed the signs to the office of Nick Santino. A collection of black and white photographs lined the cool white walls. The images were cut into artistic segments showing one piece of the Sydney Harbour Bridge, Opera House, and other historical buildings found in the central business district. A white woollen runner protected the polished marble floor and deadened my footsteps.

'Zara.'

There she was, waiting in a leather armchair by the boardroom door. My heart plunged into the pit of my stomach. I squeezed my lips together.

'Where have you been?' She tapped her gold watch.

I forced a smile. 'Mum. You're here.'

'Of course I'm here. I wouldn't miss this for the world.' Her eyes flashed, and a coolness descended on the corridor. I imagined the glass wall that bordered the waiting room cracking from the icy chill in her voice.

'I don't think it's a good idea to—'

'What are you wearing?' She rubbed the fabric of my dress between her fingers. 'You could be such a beautiful woman, if only you tried harder. Why do you always dress in a way that makes you so ... invisible?'

The comment twisted inside me like a knife, but I pushed myself to ignore it. Today was not about her.

'Because that's how I like it. Don't change the subject. Why are you here?'

'I'm just curious about what your father planned for all that money he spent his entire life making.'

'I'll tell you later,' I said with forced lightness.

My mother raised a pencilled eyebrow.

'I promise I will. So why don't you go back to the restaurant and, when I'm done here, I'll meet you there and tell you every detail.'

'Don't be ridiculous, Zara. I have every right to be here. I was married to the man for twenty-seven years.'

I crossed my arms. 'He has a name, Mum.'

'Yes, he does. You're right. Signor Selfish, Mr Tight Arse. Would you like more?'

Each word pushed a red-hot spike into my chest. My shoulders tightened with irritation. But I said nothing.

'*Andiamo*. Let's go.' She stood and strutted ahead of me into the solicitor's office.

A hush fell across the room as we entered. Wall-to-ceiling glass framed the city buildings outside. The entire room was sharp with clean lines. Minimalist. The only colour was a post-modernist painting that took up an entire wall. The erratic streaks and splashes of colour resembled the tangled nerves inside me.

The large room comfortably held four black leather chairs placed in a crescent shape around a slick glass desk. Our solicitor, Nick Santino, was sitting behind the desk in a fifth chair, whose thick silver frame was polished to a mirror finish.

Zia Rosa rushed over and, ignoring Mum, grabbed me in a wet embrace, her face damp from crying. I kissed her, one peck on each cheek.

My oldest aunt, Zia Marietta, dipped her heavily lined

eyes towards the empty chair next to her. Her lips pulled in tight as I took my seat. 'Why is she here?' she hissed in my ear.

I shrugged. Any response would fuel the bitterness between my mother and my auntie. Today needed to be about my dad. It needed to be respectful and quiet.

Zia Anna, Dad's younger sister, leaned over and squeezed my hands, her freckled face blotchy and damp with tears. She offered Mum a feeble smile and got a stony glare in return. I turned away, annoyed and embarrassed.

'Thank you for coming.' Mr Santino shook my hand warmly. 'Please accept my sincere condolences. Gennaro was a fine man.'

My mother laughed without humour.

'Leonara, this reading of the will is for those invited,' Mr Santino said, then subtly nodded at his PA, Catherine, who had been standing patiently in the corner.

Since Dad's passing, I had come to depend on Catherine. Her poise and efficiency when dealing with all the details surrounding the funeral and the will helped put me at ease. With her own measure of sophistication, Catherine was the perfect match for Leonara. She opened an adjoining door and firmly invited her to enjoy some refreshments in the private lounge.

'*Molto bene*, very good,' my mother said with an artificial smile. 'Zara, I will see you afterwards. Yes?' She glared at me as she adjusted her layered fringe.

I nodded and watched with relief as she sashayed out of the office, the tension following her out like a guileless intern.

A DULL THROBBING forced me to stop and rub my forehead. *I need coffee*, I thought, standing with a stretch. Where had the time gone?

I'd sorted all the furniture for the auction. The items, now labelled and priced, crowded the gloomy room— memories of my childhood to be sold off and owned by strangers. The past six weeks since the reading of the will had been surreal. I endured moments when my grief gripped me, but my memories were always there to provide comfort.

My stomach rumbled, and I decided to take a break. My cousin Tomasina was due any minute to help me pack away the rest of Dad's things and deliver them to St Vincent de Paul, the large charity store in the city. I could do with an ally to help with Dad's clothes and smaller mementos.

The kitchen smelled of lemon disinfectant, all evidence of family life scrubbed away by the cleaners. The wicker basket full of food Zia Anna had dropped off that morning was the only personal note in the room. Like a true Italian, she brought over her espresso machine.

'Coffee is important for such a big job.' She handed the machine over and kissed me on the cheek.

My Zias always looked after me.

I took out a large slice of lasagne, a thermos filled with homemade soup, and a bowl of green bean salad. My heart swelled when I lifted out the plate of antipasti, a careful arrangement of cheeses, olives, pickled eggplant, and zucchini. I pulled across the cling wrap and popped a garlic-infused olive in my mouth.

I looked back into the basket and smiled. Zia made fritole. My favourites. I picked one out of the container and ate it whole, licking the sugar from my fingertips.

'Way to go, Zia.' I pulled out some cutlery, a plate, and

an espresso cup. At least I didn't have to go and find the box with all the kitchen stuff in it.

I popped a coffee capsule into the espresso machine and poured some of Zia's minestrone soup into a bowl. The scent of herbs wafted out of the thermos. Standing at the sink, I dipped some olive sourdough into the soup and watched the bread soak up the aromatic broth. I twisted and turned the bread to catch any drips before rushing it into my mouth. The flavours stilled my mind for a moment.

The peace was short-lived.

Invisible. My mother's comment from all those weeks ago punctured my thoughts. A single word loaded with disappointment.

Balancing my espresso, I opened the french doors and stepped inside the sunroom—the only place in the entire house not tarnished by decades of cruel words and cold actions. Perfumed orchids, trumpet lilies, and green plants with large waxy leaves created a tropical haven. Light filtered through the glass ceiling, and candy-striped sunshine washed across the foliage. I sat in the swinging chair, sipped my coffee, and allowed the room to work its magic on me. Dad loved being in here. We'd relax together. Over coffee and a sweet treat, I'd chat about my day and he'd share tales about his former life in Vasto. As the cancer weaved through his weakened body, his kinship with Italy flourished. His obsession with my travelling to his old village grew stronger the weaker he got.

'You will love it there. It will bring you peace. *Armonia*. Harmony.' His face flushed with joy as he told me about how, as a child, he climbed cherry trees, tended goats, and swam in the sea. His hands danced higher in the air the more animated he became.

I was grateful the sunroom still provided serenity—a

space to sit with happy memories. It had always been my sanctuary when I needed a break from the turmoil of my parents' marriage. Their arguments had been spectacular. Epic. Leonara shouting with fury, her insults charging across the room.

'*Vergognoso bastardo!*'

'*Sei pazza,*' my father would lob back.

Their verbal battles usually ended with her hurling a vase, a plate, a glass—whatever she could reach—at Dad. In the beginning, these clashes sparked unbridled desire, pulling them blindly back to their marital bed.

'Having wild sex,' Tomasina had whispered to me once, when she noticed their absence after witnessing one of their fights.

Where Tomisina found their fight amusing, for me, they left a bitter taste in my mouth. Every shout and insult ripped strips off my heart. I listened with a heaviness inside me, wishing Mum would be softer. Like Dad. When—*if*—I ever found the same love that my dad tried to bestow onto my mum, I would cherish it. Always.

A month after the house had sold, my grief softened. I caught myself smiling at the memories of Dad that drifted into my thoughts. Clarity began to filter into my mind, nourishing a fleeting idea that seeded while packing up Dad's belongings. I didn't want to live in the shadow of either of my parents, especially Mum. Instead, I craved a new purpose. To live a simpler, less complicated life.

My mother told me exactly what she thought of my proposal when I'd found the courage to tell her.

'You are just like your father. *Testa dura.* Stubborn.' She'd slapped the menus down onto the bar.

'Mum, please. Don't get upset. I need to do this.'

'You want to punish me.'

The waitstaff glanced at each other as they set the tables for lunch. I ignored them.

'Oh my God, Mum. I'm not punishing you—'

'I'll be alone.'

The softness in her voice caught me off guard. I searched her face and glimpsed uncertainty in her eyes. Her past, the poverty of her childhood in the outer suburbs of Sydney, still lived inside her. What I believe haunted her was seeing my grandparents, new to Australia, work in menial jobs to survive. Jobs working with asbestos and chemicals that eventually killed them—my grandfather from cancer and my grandmother not long after. With no brothers and sisters, Leonara was alone. Vulnerable at nineteen. But she was smart and savvy. Attributes that saved and protected her. Even after marrying my father, her restaurant empire dominated.

I reached for her hand. 'Just because I loved Dad doesn't mean I don't love you.'

She snatched her hand back and busied herself with some invoices, trampling my fragile hope.

I inched forwards. 'Mum. Please. It can't always be about you.'

She looked up, eyes blazing. I knew what was coming. This time, I did what Tomasina had been begging me to do for years. I stood up to her.

'Zara—'

'No! No more. You won't be alone. You have Giorgio. Or is it Stephan? Or Luca? I don't know, Mum. Who is it this week?'

The shock on my mother's face forced me on. I needed to keep going before I lost my nerve. 'You're never alone. Dad had no one. He *was* alone.'

'*He* divorced *me*.' She flung the menus onto the floor.

'Because, *Mother*, you're the one who cheated. You're the one who broke your marital vows. You're the one who broke Dad's heart. You're why Philip went to live in Canada. You're the one who broke our family.' Tears streamed down my face.

The waitstaff had tiptoed away. If she caught them eavesdropping, Mum's wrath would be diabolical.

She was quiet.

I waited. Hoping.

Instead, she turned abruptly. 'I'm busy now.' She walked into the kitchen and summoned the head chef to discuss the specials before they opened for dinner.

I bent to pick up the scattered menus, feeling a fresh headache building behind my eyes. Then I grabbed my bag from the bar.

'When are you going?' Mum called out as I walked away.

I paused and drew in a long breath.

'Zara?' She came out of the kitchen.

'After the auction,' I said, turning around, 'Mr Santino will organise the sale of the house.'

'I'll send Robert with the car. To take you to the airport. Call me when you land.'

I nodded. Tenderness filled some of the emptiness inside me.

Underneath all the bravado—all the coolness and control, the Chanel suits, and the Botox—was a woman who loved her children. This clarity pushed hard inside my chest and my heart lurched.

What she did next floored me. She walked across the restaurant and hugged me. When she let go, she looked directly at me. 'Your father has made you and Philip very wealthy. I hated that he worked all the time ... hated that he gave all his energy to his business.' And then, more quietly, 'Hated that I was no longer the centre of his world.'

'He was only trying to make a good life for us.' I reached up and touched the top of her hand.

She pulled away. 'That wasn't enough for me, Zara. I needed great love. I needed passion. Other men could give that to me.'

I realised Mum would never change her feelings, especially when it involved Dad. I no longer wanted to fight with her. Slinging my bag over my shoulder, I kissed her, a gentle touch on both cheeks, and left, tired and depleted—yet liberated.

I'd said what I needed to. It was time to focus on the next step.

———

THE GUESTHOUSE in Vasto was owned by a middle-aged Italian woman; her outfit a throwback to the 1970s. Her bottom strained against her lime jumpsuit as she reached for my room key. I loved the reception's quirky clutter. Orange, olive, and yellow striped wallpaper added to the vintage décor. Stained cream vinyl chairs formed a circle around a low wooden table, the varnish worn at one end. Multicoloured crocheted cushions lay on each chair. The walls held plates with images of iconic Italian landmarks. Tessellated tiles, some chipped in parts, framed the receptionist's desk. The rest was gold carpet. Clean but worn over the years.

When I thought of the hotels Mum insisted we stay at in this past, this would make the Botox fall out of her face. I smiled at the thought of my mother arriving; her taut, pinched lips as she judged every inch of the place.

After settling in, I returned to the reception area and asked the woman if she'd call me a taxi. She sighed, releasing a long stream of cigarette smoke. Stubbing out the butt, she dialled. I waited as she flirted with the driver over the phone. She leaned across the counter, allowing the gold chains to escape from her ample bosom, speaking in a rapid dialect. Her head bobbed like one of those ornaments on the dashboard of a car.

'He will be here soon.' She patted her hair, a bleached copper bob sprayed stiff with cheap hairspray.

'*Grazie molte.*' The 'thank you' was laced with sarcasm. My confidence and sense of self was growing stronger each day I was away from Sydney. And my mother. There was more to me when I was away from it all. I hoped the distance and time apart might soften Mum. Make her miss having me around.

One hour later, the taxi dropped me off at the bottom of a dusty laneway. Perspiration ran down my back, soaking the band of my linen shorts. I stepped into the shade of an old cherry tree, its red fruit rotting on the ground, and gulped down warm water from a plastic bottle. The scent of provincial pine trees and wild herbs swirled around me in the heat. I unlatched an old ramshackle gate and enjoyed the relief of a light breeze brushing against me. From the stillness came a monotonous hum—possibly some kind of insect. I made a mental note to see if they sold insect spray at the pharmacy in the village.

The twenty-minute hike up the stony track worked all the muscles in my legs. I'd be sore tomorrow. And then, my heart tumbled with disappointment as my father's child-hood home came into view. The double-storey villa wasn't the monument he'd begged me to reclaim as my birthright. What stood before me was a broken and deteriorating farmhouse. Sections of the rendered walls were flayed open and exposed to the salty air. Ominous cavities loomed where windows had once been. The house sagged with melancholy and neglect.

I swallowed past the hard lump in my throat even as my flourishing confidence withered like the dry, brittle wisteria that clung to the decaying posts of the veranda.

The awning creaked and bent in submission. A rusted screen door whined on its single hinge. The sound was mournful and eerie. Something whizzed past my head and I shot up a hand to protect my face. Under the eaves was a bell-shaped beehive. The bees ignored me as they crawled over its sides, flying in and out with their bounty. Honey trickled down, making golden patterns on the brittle floorboards.

Sitting on the top step, taking care not to snag the fabric of my shorts on the splintered deck, I fought back tears. This wasn't the home my father had returned to in his memories.

What am I doing here?

I watched the dappled light move through the abandoned olive trees that flanked the house to my left. Down the valley, little white boats dotted the turquoise water of the Adriatic Sea. My breathing slowed. And then I understood it. Why Dad wanted his ashes here. Why he wanted me here.

Sitting under the eaves of the crumbling villa, bees droning in the background, I began to ponder the possibilities.

I MADE the decision to stay shortly after my arrival, while I was sitting in a bar enjoying a cappuccino and watching tourists milling about. This picturesque coastal fishing hamlet, with its neighbouring hills of wildflowers, was a haven of solace and serenity. I knew that this was where I belonged. There was nothing in Sydney to call me back. I had thought of Mum. Mum was Mum. Always would be. But the more I thought about Dad, the more my plan took shape.

The next morning, cousin Carmelina had driven me to the property on her Vespa. We left the scooter at the bottom of the laneway and strolled up to the old farmhouse.

'I have an idea,' I puffed as we hiked.

'*Dimmi*, tell me.'

'I want to use the money Dad left me to renovate the farmhouse and create a retreat for people to come and rejuvenate. To experience simplicity and to relax. Maybe they could write and paint, or reflect and heal. Enjoy the simple rural life.'

'And the farm? It's good land. It would be a shame to let it go to waste.'

I nodded. 'We could harvest olives, like the old days.' I tucked my arm into hers. 'Raise goats and make cheese to sell at the market.' Excitement tickled inside my chest. 'I want to move the beehive and have other hives. We can make our own honey.'

Carmelina stopped and scanned the horizon around the estate. Her skimpy skirt billowed against her long, tanned legs.

'What do you think?' I asked, anxiously twisting the stems of wildflowers I'd picked on the way.

'It's a good idea. I like it.'

Carmelina's enthusiasm excited me. It was all I needed to move ahead with my plans.

THERE IS a lot I could say about Italians, but over the past nine months, one thing became clear: we might be an impassioned lot, but our family bonds are unbreakable. Renovating the farmhouse to its original charm had been hard work, but Dad's presence guided me as I worked with the local tradespeople, settled into the community, and rediscovered his language. And my cousins Felice and Carmelina had been invaluable support.

After lunch, when everyone had gone for their *riposo pomeridiano*—afternoon nap—I walked through the house, marvelling at how it was coming to life. When the workmen were around, the place was filled with jovial banter and singing, but when they knocked off for their rest, the valley returned to its serene existence.

Life was slow, the ordinary moments layered with the rich. Sundays filled with large luncheons under trees. Crisp linen tablecloths covering uneven trestle tables laden with an abundance of food. Wine flowing and conversation swelling with passion and gusto. My favourite time of the day was after dinner. I'd join my aunt and cousin on their evening *passeggiata*, a stroll to help digest our food and catch up with all the gossip. I'd learned to mould my own ideals to the sedated rhythm of Vasto's provincial heart.

SITTING DOWN WITH A COFFEE, I took advantage of the quiet to catch up on some overdue invoices. With the renovations finished, I missed the buzz of activity and songs from the workmen.

As I settled in, Skype's distinct ringtone interrupted my work, and my mother's immaculate face filled the screen.

'Do you know what I received today?'

'No, but I know you're about to tell me.'

I'd written her a letter, hoping to make it more personal. Forcing her to take the time to read what I'd written and consider my invitation.

'This.' She held up my letter inviting her to visit. She was going to Genoa in two weeks to interview a Michelin-star chef for her restaurant, and I'd suggested she might like to take a detour and visit me. I'd entertained the possibility that she'd appreciate—maybe even respect—what I'd accomplished.

'I gather you won't make it?' I swallowed my disappointment.

'Darling. It was your decision to move out there, not mine. I'm sorry, but I cannot spare the time. But it is good you're enjoying your life with those people.'

'Fair enough.'

'Zara.' She leaned towards the screen. 'You know I'm busy.'

'All good, Mum. I get it.' I waved the conversation away. The months apart had changed nothing.

'*Va bene*. Be good. I must go. You look after yourself. And, Zara, try to do something about your hair. *Ciao bella*.' She hit the end button with lightning speed.

I stared at my desktop.

Maybe I was a glutton for punishment.

FELICE CALLED MY NAME.

I stepped onto the freshly painted veranda just as he brushed away some dust on the plaque. He wiped his hands on a rag and studied his handiwork.

'Perfect.' I gave him a hug.

'*É un buon nome.*' He grinned.

We stood together and admired it. It *was* a beautiful name. *Miele Viola*—Purple Honey.

I looked over to the ancient jacaranda tree, where Dad's ashes lay under a carpet of lilac. The tree's grey-brown bark mourned the loss of its flowers. Its skeletal branches spidering out towards the blue sky. I smiled, knowing that the tree would bloom again, and I wondered if, with time, my mother would allow her resentment to dissolve and learn to forgive. I shook my head and smiled. In all honesty, I knew Mum would never change.

And I was perfectly fine with that.

BOOKMARKED LETTERS

A hush fell over the library as the lunchtime crowd filtered out. Only the retired patrons remained. Some used the computers and the free internet; others settled into the single sofas to read or work on their Sudoku puzzles. The library was always popular when the weather was bitter or sweltering. Today, it was freezing outside, punishing those brave enough to venture out.

Eveline looked at the clock. Five minutes left. Irene, the head librarian, was a stickler for punctuality so Eveline started to gather up the remnants of her lunch. She didn't mind. Eveline's job for the afternoon was her favourite as a library assistant: shelving returned books into their correct spots. It was meditative. A peaceful way to finish the day.

She wrapped up her apple core in the cling wrap and popped it into her Hello Kitty lunchbox. Mrs Fiorini's chooks always looked forward to her daily scraps. She clicked the lid close and tittered at the image. Every year, her brother, Jude went out of his way to send her a quirky present for her birthday. The tradition started when they were kids. When she turned ten, he gave Eveline a mermaid brush that sang when she brushed downwards. It drove her mother mad, but she loved it. She used it every single day until the song morphed into a tired, mechanical drone. Now the brush sat on display in her living room alongside other quirky gifts: a glass bottle with a mumma duck and her duckling corked inside; and a Coco Chanel fashioned vase, complete with pearls.

When her parents came for dinner last night, Eveline giggled as she proudly showed them her latest gift—a *No Drama Llama* mug complete with the llama head as the handle. Her mother, who ran an interior design business, made it abundantly clear that she wasn't a fan of Jude's gifts.

'Eveline, why must you have these things on display? You're a grown woman. What kind of impression do you think this must make on visitors?'

'I think they're fun.' Her dad always defended her.

'They're great conversation starters!' Eveline winked at her dad.

'Darling, who would even find such objects interesting?'

Boom.

Just like that, her mum's comment sucked the oxygen out of the room.

When they left, Eveline called Jude in Amsterdam. It was late, but she needed to hear his voice.

'She just doesn't get you, Eveline.'

'*You* do. And so does Dad.'

'Yeah, but we have secret powers.'

Eveline smiled. 'Okay, what are these secret powers this time?'

'We can see brilliance in all shapes and sizes.'

EVELINE POPPED in a mint and ticked off the next item on the list in her notebook. *Lunch.* Tick.

Next on the list: afternoon shelving. She closed the notebook and popped it in her bag along with her lunchbox. She grabbed a roll of paper towels and a bottle of spray and cleaned her desk. If she got food smudges on the books, especially new ones, Irene would have kittens. She loved the scent of lavender and mint as it filled her little work nook.

The afternoon's shelving trolley was full. Eveline ran her hands along the spines and peered at the stickers, trying to figure out the most logical route around the shelves.

'Did you have a lovely break, Eveline?' Mrs Pennywell, from the retirement village down the road, peered over her gold rim glasses. She was Eveline's favourite patron who always popped in on her own when her husband was playing lawn bowls with his old army buddies.

'I did, thank you.' Eveline noticed the book tucked in between the pages of Mrs Pennywell's *Retirement Today* magazine. She narrowed her eyes curiously. 'What are you reading?'

Mrs Pennywell blushed and leaned forward to show her the book '*Fifty Shades of Grey.*'

'Oh!' The sound came out like a sneaker against a wooden floor. 'Who told you about that book?'

'All the ladies in the village. It's made quite a stir.'

Eveline grinned. 'I'm not surprised. What does Mr Pennywell think about it?'

Mrs Pennywell whispered close to Eveline. 'He doesn't know. I hide it in the laundry basket. He never goes in there. It's a safe bet.' A wide, mischievous smirk pushed her plump cheeks up.

Eveline pushed the trolley away from the reading

lounge, leaving Mrs Pennywell to enjoy her salacious book, and manoeuvred the trolley to where the 'A' authors began. She loved the repetitive and solitary action of shelving, reading the call numbers, moving books to the side, then sliding the novel in.

She picked up a copy of *Wuthering Heights*. Her favourite book. Eveline loved the classics. Sometimes, she wondered if she was born in the wrong era. Sitting at home, reading books, sewing, and taking long strolls across meadows suited her far better than trying to fit into a world that defined success by what you looked like, your job, where you lived, and your social life. Huge crowds, awkward conversations, and conflict with rude and cold people made her nervous. The three 'C's sometimes tripped her up, as Jude would say, making her feel okay about being shy around people she didn't know. Yet, living the kind of life she strove for made her heart race. There was this thrill in breaking the rules and seeing old-timey romance and a different kind of adventure, planted right here, in modern times. Maybe she was born in the right era?

Working as a library assistant was the perfect job for Eveline. She loved knowing the answers to quick-fire questions from patrons; being helpful and knowledgeable gave her pockets of small pleasures throughout the day. Her biggest joy was getting to know the regulars, especially a few of the residents, including Mrs Pennywell and a couple of mums who came each week for story time.

A battered hardback edition of *Jane Eyre* caught her eye. She lifted the book out of the shelf, and an envelope slid out and fell to the ground. She picked it up and turned it over. The envelope, made of fine paper, leaked with age. All yellow and brittle. In the top-right corner, the name 'Charlotte' was written in faded blue pen. A borrower must have used the letter as a bookmark and forgotten it when they returned the book.

She picked up the scanner on the trolley and ran it over the barcode on the back cover. No record came up. She opened the cover to check the old due date slip. REFER-ENCE ONLY was stamped across the slip in red ink.

18 June 1974—the last returned date.

This edition belonged in the antiquated book section. Strange. How did it get out in the main collection? All older and special editions were accounted for with meticulous care. Only the librarians were allowed to handle these books.

Eveline rubbed her fingers across the envelope. She felt a hard card through the paper. Turning it over, a ruby wax seal with the initials 'TP' guarded the opening.

'There you are!'

She jumped at the voice and quickly shoved the enve-lope into the pocket of her cardigan. 'I've been shelving.'

Head Librarian Irene stood at the end of the bank of shelves, her mouth pursed, and a scowl etched across her forehead.

'Yes, I can see that.' She walked over to Eveline. 'We've got a librarian meeting, and there's no milk. I need you to go down to the shop and get some. Get some Tim Tams, too. Here.' She shoved a ten-dollar note at Eveline. 'Make sure you get the receipt.' She clicked her feet and marched off.

'I reckon if that woman smiled her face would crack.'

Eveline turned to find Mrs Pennywell standing behind her. She tutted softly. 'She's just busy,' she said.

'I'm sorry, dear, but busy or not, we should never nego-tiate manners and how we speak to each other.'

A CHILL EMBRACED her as she entered her apartment. Eveline rubbed her arms and lit the fireplace. After a few pumps, the gas caught, and flames ran across the rocks. The fake fireplace was a present from Jude for her birthday two years ago—his most (and only) sensible gift.

'No quirky birthday presents for your eighteenth. This is a reprieve. You only get three. Eighteenth, twenty-first, and fiftieth. Milestones should always be marked with lavish gifts from a big brother.'

'Or is it so I go and tell everyone how great my big brother is?' Eveline grinned at him.

'That too,' Jude said as he brushed his shoulder.

Although Eveline loved Jude's funny and impractical gifts, this present was perfect. Her apartment, built in the 1940s, was draughty and cold in winter.

She popped the kettle on and went to hang up her coat in the bedroom. Her heart melted. Fern lay in a puddle of blankets, his dark grey paw across his face. At the sound of her entering the room, he stirred and looked over at Eveline. His bright blue eyes danced with affection. In the cat world, Fern was a beauty.

'Well, hello. Look what you've done to my freshly made bed.'

Fern walked over for a head butt; his feline kiss.

Eveline picked him up and carried him into the kitchen where the kettle was whistling.

'It's warmer out here. I'm going to have a nice cup of tea, and then we'll have dinner.'

As she sat on the sofa, she remembered the envelope. She reached into her pocket and pulled it out, turning it over and over in her hands. Eventually, her curiosity got the better of her. She held the envelope up to the light. There was definitely a card inside.

Should she? No. It's someone's private business. But she wanted to. The letter intrigued her.

Jude. She'd ask Jude. She checked her phone—6.14 p.m. —morning in Amsterdam.

She put him on speaker while she made dinner.

'Hello. Can I ask you something?'

'Am I the cleverest brother in the world?'

'Yes, but I have another question.'

'Shoot.'

'I found this envelope. It fell out of a book. They wrote the name 'Charlotte' in the top right-hand corner. And there's a wax seal, red, with the initials 'TP'.'

'This doesn't sound like a standard lost property issue.'

'It was inside a copy of *Jane Eyre,* which was returned in 1974. That's nearly fifty years ago.' Eveline picked up the envelope. 'I want to open it. Is that wrong?' The words tumbled out fast.

Silence.

'Jude? Am I a bad person?'

She heard Jude take a long breath and let it out.

'I am, aren't I?'

'I'm thinking.'

Eveline waited. Jude was a deep thinker and liked to mull an idea around before he decided.

'The way I see it, people find letters from the past all the time. In a small way, they're a part of history. Don't you think?'

Eveline nodded. 'History. Yes. I never thought of it that way. Maybe something significant for this area.'

'Exactly. Also, you might be able to return it to the rightful owner. They'd appreciate it.'

'Okay. So, I should ... *can* ... open it?'

'Eveline, you're the kindest, sweetest girl. I know you'd treat this with care.'

She chatted with Jude about what she'd been up to since the last time they spoke. It wasn't much. She went to work, came home, and spent Sunday night having dinner with with mum and dad. Jude always had something interesting to say, and she loved hearing the stories of the people he met and the places he went.

Once she hung up, Eveline grabbed a sharp steak knife and ran it along the top edge of the envelope to open it. The paper was thin, and she took her time.

She pulled out a card and read the note.

DEAR CHARLOTTE,

I know you love treasure hunts. This is one I created just for you. Now you know why I encouraged you to read Jane Eyre. *If you have this card, you took my advice. Why* Jane Eyre? *You and the author are connected.*

Do you know how?

EVELINE PAUSED.

Charlotte.

The note was addressed to Charlotte and Charlotte Brontë wrote *Jane Eyre*.

'This isn't too difficult,' she said to Fern, who lay across the bench, his legs dangling. She kept reading.

FOR YOUR NEXT *clue you need to find:*

'And then my heart with pleasure fills,
And dances with daffodils.'

Love, Thomas

EVELINE KNEW THE LINE. It was from Wordsworth's poem, 'Daffodils.'

———

EVELINE OPENED the library and shivered. The icy night air penetrated every corner. She started an hour before the library opened to the public and thirty minutes before the three librarians arrived. Her job was to prepare the library. She turned on the air conditioner (already set to warm), filled the kettle with water and turned it on, tidied the circulation desk, powered on all the computers, and opened all the blinds.

She checked her watch. Ten minutes before anyone else arrived. Pulling out her notebook and a pen, she turned to today's list. Food scraps to Mrs Fiorini's chickens. Tick. Breakfast and washed bowl. Tick. Air con, kettle, computers —tick, tick, tick.

Eveline pulled the envelope out of her cardigan pocket and stared down at it, as if still deciding.

As if she hadn't already decided.

Her mouth set, she walked over to the poetry section and pulled out *The Selected Poems of William Wordsworth*.

She couldn't believe it.

There was another letter inside. The same kind.

Eveline rushed over to the shelving trolley and scanned the barcode. Last borrowed, June 1972.

She grabbed a knife from the kitchen and slid it under the seal to open it.

.   .   .

DEAR CHARLOTTE,

Congratulations on finding this second card. I knew it wouldn't be difficult. I know how much you love 'Daffodils.'

What do you affectionally call your William Wordsworth?

Eveline read the question again. '*Your* William Wordsworth.' She tapped the letter against her hand. The note was signed Thomas, and she couldn't see or make the connection. 'Affectionally call...' she muttered. Her dad called her Evie when he was being affectionate with her.

'Will! Well, Miss Charlotte, you're quite friendly with our esteemed Mr Wordsworth.'

She read on.

The next clue is: To Kill a Mockingbird. *Atticus is not alone in fighting for Tom.*

Love, Thomas

EVELINE FOUND THE NOVEL. Three copies, three different editions sat on the shelf. Nothing in the first, nor the second...nor the third. Disappointment gripped her heart. Someone must have borrowed it and found the note. She put the books back, took out the note, and re-read the clue. *Who helped Atticus?* The study notes might have the answer. She remembered the part where Atticus set up camp outside Tom's cell when he heard there might be a lynching mob. She raced to the shelves where the modern copies of *To Kill a Mockingbird* and the study guides lived. Collecting all the copies off the shelf, she sat on the floor. Eveline flicked the pages, sending wisps of air in her direction as she turned to the list of characters—*Baxton Bragg Underwood, Maycomb's newspaper editor.*

'Underwood, Underwood,' Eveline muttered. Then it hit her. 'Under *wood. Under what?*'

She knelt to pick up the scattered copies and returned the books. Slowly, she looked underneath the shelf.

Nothing.

Eveline stood and thought. *To Kill a Mockingbird. Underwood.* 'Of course!' She raced back to where the first edition copies sat on the shelf. Tentatively, she looked under the wooden shelf.

Her heart pinged. A letter. The tape, now aged and brittle, cracked as she pulled it away. 'Under the shelf!' She chuckled. 'Tom, you are one clever man.'

EVELINE HOPED she could sneak a peek inside the envelope, but the library buzzed with patrons all day. It seemed as though everyone who lived near the library visited. She barely had time to eat some morning tea.

She decided to have lunch at Bee's Knees Café down the street. This would give her some privacy to open the third letter, and the hot homemade scones beckoned her.

EVELINE SETTLED at a table in the corner that looked out onto the street. After she ordered, she pulled the envelope out of her cardigan and used the knife set at the table to slice through an opening. She pulled out another card.

DEAR CHARLOTTE,

Well done. I knew you would be clever and find the third card.

Do you remember about the mumma sheep? You cried in my arms, and I fell in love with you deeper. Your kindness to animals makes me love you more.

On to the next and final clue. A Jane Austen story. One that shares your middle name. Look for the chapter that has the same number as my hometown team in San Francisco.

Love, Thomas

EVELINE SIPPED HER CAPPUCCINO. She knew the story and remembered the scene. The young farmer loses his sheep when dogs chase them over a cliff. She'd studied it in year ten English, but that was a while ago now. Tapping her fingers on the side of the cup, she looked out the window.

Do you remember about the mumma sheep?

Eveline watched a man wrestle with his umbrella.

Do you remember about the mumma sheep?

'Of course!'

Her hands shot into the air in celebration, knocking the table and sending coffee everywhere. Grabbing the serviettes, Eveline mopped up the mess, feeling the whole café's eyes on her.

'It's okay. It's not a café if we don't get at least one spillage per day.' The waitress hurried over and helped to clean the table with a sturdier cloth. 'Sounds like you solved a problem.' She smiled. Her eyes held a friendly warmth to them.

'Thank you. I have. *Part* of the problem, anyway.'

'Sounds intriguing. My name's Meg.' She held out her hand.

She shook it. 'Eveline.'

Meg pulled the chair opposite and sat. Her confidence and close proximity sent a tingle up Eveline's spine, and she shuffled in her seat.

'So, care to share? I need a little excitement in my life.'

Meg's full laugh and the way the wrinkles deepened around her brown eyes, put Eveline at ease. A few strands of grey hair crept up her fringe. Eveline estimated she was about the same age as her mum. Around fifty.

'Won't you get in trouble sitting here?'

'Me? No. This is my café. Tara over there is my daughter. She can handle things for a bit.' Meg scanned the café. 'The mid-morning crowd is done for today, thank goodness. When it's cold we get busy as ... well ... bees.' She let out another laugh.

Eveline liked Meg. She was bursting to share the—well, what could she call it? Treasure hunt? Scavenger hunt?

'I work at the library shelving returned books. And I discovered these letters. I think they were written fifty years ago.' She pulled out the first two notes and offered them to Meg.

Meg flipped the envelopes over, her eyes sparkling. 'Beautiful seal. You don't see those these days.'

'You don't see letters much, either.' Eveline sighed. She gestured for Meg to open them. 'You can read them.'

Eveline watched as Meg read. She was bursting with excitement to find out what she thought.

Meg handed the letters back. 'Intriguing.'

'I think so too.' Eveline loved that someone else found this fascinating. 'The first letter led me to a collection of poetry with 'Daffodil' in it – that's the poem he quoted.'

'Not one for reading poetry, but I can see that. And that's where you found the second letter?'

'Yep! The clue for that was 'Will' – as in short for 'William.' She passed the third envelope to her. 'Then it led me to this one.'

Meg shook her head. 'I'm lost.'

'Mumma sheep. Female. Female sheep are *ewes*.'

'Ewe – as in, *you*!' Meg cried out. 'Oops, that was loud.' She smiled apologetically at the two people having a meeting at the next table.

'Do you know the next one? It's something about Austen and a name.'

'I'm afraid I'm not into old-fashioned books. I prefer detective mysteries myself. But it's a title with a girl's name, if I understand it correctly. Do you know Austen's titles? All I can remember is *Pride and Prejudice*. I saw the BBC series on Netflix a couple of years ago.'

'She also wrote *Sense and Sensibility* and—' Eveline gasped. '*Emma!*' But then, she sighed. 'It's not enough to know the title, though. He writes '*Look for the chapter that has the same number as my hometown team in San Francisco.*' Football's *not* my thing.'

Meg picked up the card. 'Hey, Tara, what's the name of that football team in San Francisco?'

'The 49ers,' the man at the next table offered.

'Thanks, Roy. See, it always pays to get to know your customers.' Meg winked at Eveline.

'The 49ers. Chapter forty-nine in *Emma*.' Eveline laughed. This was getting exciting.

THE AFTERNOON PLODDED ON. Eveline checked her watch and jumped up. 'Thanks for your help.' She picked up the letters and popped them in her bag.

Eveline raced into the library.

'You're late,' Irene hissed at her.

Eveline glanced at the clock. She had two more minutes.

'I'm sorry. I can lock up to make up the time?'

'Just this once.' Irene pushed her thick tortoiseshell glasses back up her nose and trundled to her office underneath the library.

Eveline didn't mind about closing. She had nothing else on after work. And besides, it would give her the perfect opportunity to look for the copy of *Emma* and find the next and final clue.

THE HARD-CORE REGULARS were always the last to leave. Eveline stood at the open door, saying goodbye, and trying not to look too impatient for them all to be gone.

'Good afternoon, Mrs Pennywell. Say hi to Mr Pennywell. I've missed him this week.' Eveline pulled her cardigan tight across her chest, keeping out the chilly afternoon breeze.

Mrs Pennywell squeezed her arm in thanks as she passed. 'He's not feeling the best. I put my foot down and told him he wasn't to venture out in this bitter cold. But I think I've cleaned you out of thrillers.' She held up a basket full of books.

'That looks heavy. Why don't you wait, and I'll carry them back with you?'

Looking for the next clue could wait.

'Oh, no. My daughter's just outside.'

Mrs Pennywell waved at a sophisticated woman in a tailored blue suit and cream coat. 'That's Tessa. She's an investment banker. Very fancy job.' Mrs Pennywell lifted her shoulders and smiled.

'You must be very proud of her.'

'I am. We both are.'

Eveline's heart twinged. Little bubbles of sadness escaped. For a moment, she wished for the same sentiment from her mum. She sighed and pushed the thoughts deep down. They were safer locked away.

Eveline waited until Mrs Pennywell and Tessa turned the corner. She bolted the double glass doors and pulled the blinds across.

When everything looked perfect, she unlocked the door to the antiquated books and headed to the fiction section.

Eveline pulled down a copy of *Emma* and settled on one of the reading couches. She flicked to chapter forty-nine and started reading. Mr Knightly proposes to Emma. But she says she can't. She must look after her father.

Eveline grabbed a pen and paper out of the scrap paper tray left for people to make notes. She wrote: *Will - ewe (You)*. She looked at chapter forty-nine. Of course. Easy-peasy. *Will you marry me?* Thomas was asking Charlotte to marry him. How romantic.

The realisation hit her.

Charlotte never got the letters. Eveline found them sealed. She may never have known what Thomas had planned. Did he ever propose? What was her answer? Did she say yes? Did they live happily ever after?

Eveline slumped down. How disappointing. Someone out there named Thomas tried to propose to a girl named Charlotte through classical literature. What a shame it never happened. Instead, the notes sat hidden for nearly fifty years.

She bundled the letters together, pulled the green

ribbon out of her ponytail, and tied the notes together with a tight bow. 'That's that,' she said to the bundle.

Collecting her coat and bag, she popped the letters inside her desk, tucked inside an old Quality Street tin she had bought at the last library fête. The disappointment pressed down hard inside her.

Outside, the grey, soppy weather matched her mood.

THAT NIGHT, Eveline called Jude.

'What's up? Trouble with Mum?'

'No.'

'Work?'

'In a way. You know that letter?'

'The one you found in the library book?'

'I found three more.'

The phone went silent.

'Evie?'

A sniff escaped and the emotion startled her. Thinking that Charlotte may never have gotten the letters made her heart quiver.

'Life's not perfect, is it?'

'Not always. But sometimes, it does surprise you.'

'I think life is fragile with all these cracks that threaten to make things worse.'

'Yet, the cracks let some light through.'

Eveline wiped her tears from her cheek with the back of her hand. 'You're really wise, Jude.'

'All big brothers are. It's our job.'

Eveline told Jude all about the letters and the clues they held. He told her that if two people were meant to be together, they would find each other. When Eveline said goodnight, she felt better. She sent a little wish out to the universe, hoping Thomas didn't give up and somehow, he and Charlotte did marry and lived happily ever after.

EVELINE FINISHED HANGING up the crepe paper flowers for the Spring Read display. Sprinkles of sunshine beamed down and warmed the reading corner. The cerulean sky lay unblemished above.

'That looks lovely.'

Eveline turned around.

'Mrs Pennywell! We've missed you. How's Mr Pennywell? Is he okay?'

Mrs Pennywell's pale blue eyes filled with tears, and she shook her head.

'Oh no.' Eveline ushered the woman to the sofa and put a careful arm around her. She didn't care what Irene would say about her sitting down when she should be working. They were a community library—the hub of their town—and one of their own needed support.

'What happened?'

Mrs Pennywell reached into her handbag, pulled out a handkerchief, and dabbed her eyes. 'He passed last week. The funeral was a few days ago. I needed a change of scenery and my daughter Tessa's gone back home to her job in the city. I need to escape in some stories. Read the books we used to love. All the classics.' Mrs Pennywell paused and smiled. 'You know, Thomas got me into Jane Austen and the Brontës when we were courting. It was the early seventies. Even though the world was filled with exciting new things, Thomas always had a passion for the classics. Always content to bury himself in romantic literature.'

Thomas. The name flashed in Eveline's mind. Written on yellowing paper with faded blue ink.

A few times over the past six weeks, Eveline had pulled the letters out and re-read them. They always brought a sigh, knowing how much Thomas loved Charlotte. But it also made her sad that Charlotte never experienced his proposal. Life was never perfect.

Slowly, the connection fused inside her mind. The Pennywells' love of Austen and the Brontës. Was it possible?

'Mrs Pennywell, do you have a favourite poet as well?'

'I do. Why do you ask?'

'Just wondering. Would it, by any chance, be Wordsworth?'

The look on Mrs Pennywell's face told Eveline all she needed to know. Before she could stop herself, she blurted out, 'Is your first name Charlotte?'

'Yes, it is. Why—'

Eveline's hand flew up to her mouth and she gasped. An elderly man reading the daily paper glanced over and threw Eveline an irritated look. She ignored it and raced to her desk in the workroom, leaving a stunned Mrs Pennywell in her wake.

She returned with the tin clasped in her hands. She smiled at the confused Mrs Pennywell and took out the bundle of letters. Her heart was racing like a puppy chasing a butterfly.

'I have something that I believe belongs to you.'

TREASURES OF THE HEART

Frankie held the box on her lap. Every time the car hit a pothole, she winced and peeked inside to make sure the items were safe. They weren't expensive, but they were precious. Retro bits and bobs that she'd collected over the decades. Maybe some would be of interest to Gumtree enthusiasts.

Who are these people making a living selling second-hand items? she thought. *Stay-at-home mums*, she assumed. Women who'd left fast-paced careers in boardrooms and were itching to use their talents and expertise. Frankie *tsked* out loud, reprimanding herself for being so bitchy. She knew it was coming from a place of jealousy.

Allyson reached over from the driver's seat and grabbed her hand. 'Are you okay?'

'Yeah.' Frankie let out a long sigh. 'I really wanted to tell Nan she was going to be a great-grandma.'

'Listen, it isn't over till the fat lady sings, and this fat lady is ready to belt out a tune. There's a tap dance on a loop inside my head.'

Frankie sighed. 'You know that's not the right context.'

'It isn't?'

'Nope. It means it's nearly over.'

'Shit! Sorry. I've been saying it wrong all these years. People must've been laughing behind my back.'

Frankie placed her hand on Allyson's arm. 'I know what you meant.'

Allyson brushed Frankie's cheek. 'I love you.' She moved her hand to change gears. 'Do you think people have been laughing at me?'

'Absolutely,' Frankie chuckled.

Allyson poked her tongue out.

'BUT I WANTED to give you a baby too,' Frankie said quietly.

'Look,' Allyson said, giving her hand a squeeze, 'there's no reason we can't use your egg in my oven. Who cares who carries the baby?'

'I love your positivity. I'd like some, please.' Frankie lifted Allyson's hand and kissed a freckled knuckle, marvelling once again at her love's slender hands and impeccable nails. 'By the way, when the fat lady sings it's nearly over.'

Allyson smiled, keeping her eyes on the road. 'Yeah. When you have a baby all those doubts of yours will be gone. *Arrivederci.*'

'Nice save.'

Tall and curvaceous, Allyson had always reminded Frankie of a heroine in a French noir film. They met at a life-drawing class, where they admired and critiqued each other's work with comfortable ease. Their friendship blossomed when they started drinking boutique beer after class. Allyson's old schoolmate ran a hip alley bar, and they became regulars every Thursday night. Their friendship shed its polite armour during the second semester, revealing intense feelings. Frankie had never been happier in a relationship.

The car jostled again, causing the box's contents to tinkle.

'Sorry,' Allyson said. 'I can understand why people want to live near the coast, but you'd think they'd pave the road.'

'Nan never allowed it,' Frankie said, her tone tinged with pride. 'She knew that a decent road brings commercial development. She became an expert, and a fixture in front of the council.'

'She sounds feisty. I wonder who takes after her?' Allyson grinned.

'Hilarious.' Frankie swatted Allyson's knee.

They fell into comfortable silence as Allyson drove through a tunnel of eucalyptus and banksia trees. Frankie loved this part of the journey. Her very own enchanted world, complete with a scalloped bay, soft under foot with translucent sand and framed by iridescent water. As a child, she'd spent long summer days making sandcastles, playing in the rock pools, and collecting shells. She could almost taste the cold, sticky watermelon and frozen grapes Nan always packed for a day at the beach.

'Are you okay?' Allyson asked, pulling her out of her thoughts.

'Just worried. I don't know how much Nan's remembering these days. Dad said to prepare myself. What does that even mean?'

'I think it means just that,' Allyson said, and turned into the driveway. She stopped at the gate.

Frankie released the seatbelt, leaned over, and kissed her. 'I love you.'

'You better.'

Stepping out of the car, Frankie inhaled the briny air—the cicadas' symphony proof that summer had settled in.

'If you could bottle it, you'd solve all the world's woes,' Nan had always said about coastal living.

Frankie opened the gate and waited until the bush turkeys scuttled away. Allyson drove slowly through while Frankie opened the mailbox. A sadness descended as she pulled out copies of the local paper and letters stained with damp spots.

She closed the gate and ran back to the car. Frankie got in and shook the mail at Allyson. 'She's been on her own for a while,' she said, her voice wobbling.

'We're here now. Focus on that.' Allyson drove carefully around a large pothole. 'Sweetie, you can't change the past. You *have* to stop beating yourself up.'

'But—' Frankie stopped. She knew Allyson was right. She had to stop dumping on herself. All this negativity was doing her head in: her obsession with falling pregnant, her guilt for not being around for Nan, her shame for not calling her dad more often. If only she'd spent the last twelve months being *present* for everyone ...

The thought sent her spiralling again.

Picturing Nan here alone, after Pop died, was like a punch to the base of her throat. The panic surged through her veins. If her mum were around, she would've prodded Frankie to visit her nan. She'd always gotten everyone to do the right thing in her caring, non-aggressive way. She'd throw out a casual 'I wonder how Nan's doing' or a 'Nan was asking after you—it'll make her day if you took a trip up the coast'. No judgement in her tone. Just a passing thought —enough to plant a seed in Frankie's mind.

The years had dulled the pain of losing her mum but

hadn't taken it away. At least her dad was doing okay. He'd picked up his life and was dating a nice lady. Nan was his mum-in-law, but he still called each month to catch up and check she was okay. It was her dad who'd initially been worried about Nan's memory. He'd broken the news to Frankie over coffee the day after Nan's results came in.

'How're all those wedding plans?' he'd asked, after they'd settled themselves at a table.

'Easy. Allyson's doing most of it and loving it.'

'I'm glad she's going to make a respectable woman out of you.'

Frankie chuckled. 'Wow, Dad. Maybe I'll make a respectable woman out of *her*.' Her father cocked an eyebrow. 'Yeah, you're right.' She laughed.

'Always am, Frannikins.' He smiled. But Frankie knew something was up when he took her hand. 'Listen. I don't want to worry you, but I rang Nan last week, and ... well, she started telling me she was worried about Pop, saying he'd gone out for a surf and hadn't come back.'

'Out for a surf? But Pop's been gone ...' She trailed off, knowing exactly what her dad was about to tell her.

Frankie sat and listened, her heart tearing itself into pieces.

'It was odd. Rebecca and I took a drive and found the place in shambles. Dirty dishes in the sink, an uncooked beef rump on the bench—riddled with maggots—and the poor chickens desperate for food. Most of their eggs had gone off. How the foxes didn't kill the hens is a wonder.'

'Why didn't you tell me?'

'You've had enough on your plate.' He hesitated. 'You know, with the miscarriages.'

'You should've told me,' Frankie said forcefully, to stop herself from breaking down.

'She's good now.' Her dad laid his hand on her forearm. 'We've organised care for her, and a housekeeper goes in daily. But her memory's fading. I think it'll help her to have family around.'

Frankie didn't need to be convinced. This was her nan. Who'd loved her unconditionally. Who'd cried with her and held her when her mum died, and who told her stories to keep her mum's memory alive. Now, Nan's memory was eroding. How could life be so cruel?

A few days ago, Frankie called her nan's GP. She wanted to ask if there was anything she could do to help her. Dr Jamieson encouraged them to find objects that would help trigger memories.

Allyson parked under a flame tree. Frankie barely waited for the car to stop before she leaped out and ran up the front steps. To her relief, the house smelled clean. A delicate scent of eucalyptus filled the hallway.

'Hello? Nan?'

'She's napping.' A woman in a sky-blue uniform stepped out from the living room. 'You must be Frankie.'

'Yes. You are?'

'Yvonne. Maggie's carer.'

'Of course. Yes. Dad told me.'

Allyson entered behind Frankie and handed her the box. 'You left it in the car.'

Frankie reached up and placed a hand on her cheek. 'I was so eager to see Nan.'

'I know.' Allyson gave her a warm smile.

Over tea and fruitcake in the kitchen, Yvonne explained that Nan was still experiencing some good days, though the prognosis wasn't great. A nursing home was inevitable. Frankie wept while Allyson asked all the right questions and wrote down the responses. *Once a PA, always a PA*, Frankie thought with gratitude.

After her nap, Nan wandered in dressed in casual clothes. Her hair was neat in her usual bun, and Frankie could smell her signature perfume: Estée Lauder's Youth Dew. She relaxed as soon as she saw her nan's face light up at the sight of her. Today was a good day.

She and Allyson took Nan down to the beach. At seventy-five, the woman was still physically fit. The fact was bitter-sweet. After a swim, they strolled along the beach. The sun dried their wet bathers, leaving a dusting of salt on their skin. Frankie's stomach lurched as they collected shells, just as they'd done when she was a kid. After walking the beach's length, they sat under the speckled canopy of an ancient Moreton Bay fig tree, popping grapes in their mouths between stories and wiping away watermelon juice as it ran down their chins.

'Sorry they're not frozen,' Allyson said.

Frankie's heart almost burst with affection. Allyson always remembered the smallest details. She made the shitty parts of life bearable.

Back at the house, Frankie and Nan sat on the sweeping veranda enjoying the summer breeze while Allyson went for another swim. The view of the beach was breathtaking and unspoilt. The rolling ocean always made Frankie feel small as it stretched towards the horizon.

Whenever the conversation came to a natural end, Frankie would hurriedly find another topic. She knew if she stopped talking, the tears would come.

Finally, Nan looked at her sadly and stroked her hair. 'Frankie, I know what's happening.'

'You do?' Frankie swallowed.

'I know that some days I disappear.' Soft creases appear

around her faded grey eyes as she gives Frankie a small, sad smile. 'But I sense I'm okay. I *feel* the love, though it feels like I'm under water. Sounds and images are blurry sometimes.'

Frankie held Nan's hands, noticing that they were well kept, manicured with a light pink polish. The wrinkles rippled to her wrist. How was she going to cope without her?

Nan reached over and gave Frankie a hug. 'Yvonne's very good. Honest and straight to the point. I'm well looked after.'

Frankie stopped trying to hold back her tears. 'I'm sorry,' she sniffed. 'I'm trying to be brave.'

'Why?' Nan gathered Frankie into a hug. 'Life's hard. And a bloody bugger too.'

Frankie smiled. 'You've always been such a rock. All I've done is wallow because I can't carry a baby and Allyson can. She can carry my egg, as well as hers, when she's ready, so in many ways we're so much luckier than a lot of people. But all I can think about is how I'm missing out on the complete experience.'

Nan tucked a strand of hair around Frankie's ear. 'Life is about collecting experiences and they come in all shapes and sizes. Just because a baby doesn't grow inside you doesn't mean it won't be loved.' She turned to look at Allyson who was walking through the wash. 'I can see how much you two love each other. I know that love will flow to your little baby, regardless of who carries it. It will still be a part of you.' Nan let out a soft sigh. 'I've lived a long life, and if there's one thing I've learned it's that you need to take the joy, in whatever package it comes in.'

Nan reached for the box on the table in front of them. 'Like these items. All pieces of memories.' Nan took out the bag of shells. 'Each one of these represents a wonderful moment in *your* life, too, not just mine. We spent many years walking along the beach and collecting these shells.' She held up a glossy cowrie shell with leopard spots. 'The same experience but wrapped in a different memory.' She smiled warmly at Frankie. 'Does it matter when and how memories are collected? They still happen.'

Nan looked out to where Allyson was now swimming. 'She loves you. And I know you love her. Make babies. Make plenty of them if you wish. It doesn't matter who carries them. Each child will be a part of your life. A part of your memories. And I will live in theirs, as I do with you.'

Frankie hugged Nan. 'I love you.'

'I know. And that's the one thing that I hang on to whenever my mind goes walkabout,' she said with a laugh. 'Love is and will always be the most wonderful thing in our lives. If you remember nothing else, remember that.'

THANK YOU FOR READING MY BOOK!

If you enjoyed the stories in this anthology, and I'm hoping you did, I would love it (truthfully, I'd be tinkled pink) if you'd be willing to spare just two to three minutes to leave me an honest, authentic review. This well help other potential readers like you find out about this book.

YOU CAN LEAVE a review on your favourite online book store, including Goodreads.

IF YOU'VE ALREADY LEFT a review, you're wonderful, and I can't thank you enough!

GLOSSARY

I'm an Australian writer, who grew up with an Italian heritage. My mother migrated from Sicily in 1960 and my father from Istria in 1959. The stories in this anthology have come from my imagination and are delivered to you in an Aussie voice, fashioned from an Australian/Italian culture with Greek friends—and from watching loads of movies.

There are some words that are distinctly part of the Australian vernacular and so I have created this glossary to help you gain more clarity as a reader.

I HAVE ALSO TRANSLATED the Italian and Greek words and phrases used in the stories. Although any words in another language are framed in the context of dialogue, I thought this extra information would allow you to develop a stronger understanding of the languages and cultures these stories represent.

. . .

AUSTRALIAN TERMS

bugger – used as an exclamation of alarm or concern, e.g. 'Oh bugger, I dropped my beer!'

cockatoo – a white parrot with a yellow crest

Fat Yak, Stone and Wood, 150 Lashes, Little Creatures – all boutique beers

footy – Rugby League (see below). A form of rugby

Jacaranda Tree a tree that blooms purple flowers in late spring. Origin from Brazil

morning tea - a light snack and/or drink taken at mid morning, before lunch, especially during a work or school break.

punter – a customer of a commercial establishment. This slang word also drills down deeper and is also referred to loosely as an informal member of society, an everyman.

Rugby League – a form of rugby with thirteen players a side

State of Origin – a Rugby League competition between the states of New South Wales and Queensland. The best of three games wins the trophy

Wag – to skip school. Be a truant

ITALIAN TERMS

acqua passata non macina piu – pure water no longer grinds / water that's flowed past the mill grinds no more

andiamo – here we go / let's go / come

armonia – harmony

chi si volta, e chi si gira, sempre a casa va finire – who turns around, and who turns around, always ends up at home *ciao bella* – hi, beautiful

ciao, dolcezza – hello, sweetie

dimmi – tell me

disgraziata – unfortunate

é un buon nome – it's a good name

fritole – deep fried dumplings / donuts with sprinkled sugar on top

gli e´ mancato la sua famiglia – he missed his family

grazie – thank you

grazie molte – thank you very much

la dolce vita – the sweet life

mia cara – my dear (feminine)

mio caro – my dear (masculine)

miele viola – purple honey

molto bene – very good

nonna – grandmother

Padre nostro, Ave Maria, Gloria al Padre, Sacro Cuore di Gesù, ripongo tutta la mia fiducia in te – Our Father, Hail Mary, Glory to the Father, Sacred Heart of Jesus, I place all my trust in you

passeggiata – walk / a stroll

perche – why

riposo pomeridiano – afternoon rest

sei pazza – you are crazy

si – yes

silenzio – silence

sta attento a cosa desideria – be careful what you want / be careful what you wish for

testa dura – stubborn

ti amo – I love you

un incanto – an enchantment

un orologio astromomico – an astronomic watch

una cimaurta – an Italian amulet worn around the neck or hung to ward off the evil eye

una pecora nero – a black sheep

una ragazza forte – a strong girl

va bene – all right

vergognoso bastardo – shameful bastard

voi un café – want a coffee

voi un café con biscotti – want a coffee with a biscuit

zia – aunty

zio – uncle

GREEK TERM

yiayia – grandmother

ACKNOWLEDGMENTS

There are so many people to thank. This anthology of short stories represents the start of my publishing career. One where I no longer write stories to read to myself, then file them away in the bottom drawer of my desk. I love writing short stories. They allow me to grab all the characters in my head and breathe life into them through my words. These stories are snapshots in my characters' lives, and I am privileged to give them a voice.

I want to thank my wonderful and dedicated team of beta readers: Seodin Hevey, Michelle Dowling, Danielle Toffoli, Julie Monaghan, Stuart Brownscombe, and Kelly Redhead-Adelt. These were the first readers to look at my stories with a reader's eye and give me valuable, authentic feedback, and they never held back—in short, exactly what a writer needs to make sure their stories work.

These stories sing because of my editors. Rachel Small, whose work on the developmental editing ensured the stories shone. Elanor Best, for the extensive copy edits that pushed me outside my boundaries, making the stories sparkle even more. Lottie Clemens and Elise Gallagher, my proofreaders, who ensured not one comma, word, or sentence was out of place and to ensure the reading experience kept you in the story and not focused on any typos.

I want to thank my husband Tim and daughter Caitlin, who support me in my writing. The creative pursuit requires you to spend time alone, but they were always waiting for me to emerge, for yet another espresso, to share some of my writing, or for human connection and conversation. I love you both dearly, and I could not do this without you.

Finally, to my cats Miss Lily and Daisy and my dog Mischa for being my constant writing companions.

THANK YOU FOR READING MY BOOK!

If you enjoyed the stories in this anthology, and I'm hoping you did, I would love it (truthfully, I'd be tinkled pink) if you'd be willing to spare just two to three minutes to leave me an honest, authentic review. This well help other potential readers like you find out about this book.

YOU CAN LEAVE A REVIEW ON:
Amazon
Goodreads

IF YOU'VE ALREADY LEFT a review, you're wonderful, and I can't thank you enough!

WANT MORE SHORT STORIES?

As a thank you for reading my stories, I would love to offer you three additional stories, plus a bonus fifth story I wrote for an assignment in my Master of Letters in Creative Writing.

Click on the image below to sign up and receive your additional stories!

Go to https://www.valeriegmiller.com/some-days-anthology

COMING IN 2022

A brand-new novel and novella!
Want to know more? Sign up to my monthly emails.
Go to www.valeriegmiller.com and subscribe

AUTHOR INTERVIEW

When did you start writing?

Maybe the question should be, when did I start telling stories? When I was little, before I could write, I used to look at the images in picture books and make up stories. As soon as I could string a decent sentence together in English, I started to write stories. When I was in primary school, my mum would buy me a lined exercise book and I would write the story on the right-hand side and draw a coloured illustration on the left-hand side.

How do you handle writer's block?

I go for a walk and let my mind wander. I find getting lots of sleep and making sure I eat nourishing foods helps. Just stopping to fill my creative well helps, too. I do this by reading, watching movies, or taking photos. Sometimes I leave the work and go on to another project. I always have three to four writing projects, at different stages, on the go at the same time.

What comes first, the characters or the plot?

Always the characters. The plot develops from them. I always start with a distinct image of the main female protagonist in my mind.

When did you consider yourself a writer?

When my first short story was published in an online literary magazine. Several authors have said, 'If you write, then you're a writer.' I believe this, too.

Describe your writing space.

I live in an apartment with my husband and daughter (who will move out…one day!) and have full reign of the study at the end of the apartment. It has an image board, framed photos from my travels overseas, Post-it notes everywhere, piles of books, my notebooks, and research material for each story. A bookshelf filled with craft books stands behind my desk. I love fashion and architecture, especially Art Deco buildings, and have coffee books on all these subjects to inspire me. There's a rug for my dog who loves to lie at my side, and there's always a cat asleep next to, or behind, my laptop. The study has no door, but I purchased a 'Writer at Work' sign to display, so my family knows when I'm working.

What time of day do you write?

I discovered that early morning is the optimum time to write my first draft. I'm still working full-time at a school where I teach English. I get up at 4 a.m. and write until 6.30 a.m. Then I take the dog for a walk and get ready for work. When I get home, I read for an hour. This gets my creative headspace switched on. I always do all my edits after work, and then I plan and plot the next book on the couch with my family as they watch TV. I do all my plotting and planning the old-fashioned way: by hand in a notebook, cutting out images and pasting them in with glue, and using coloured pencils, highlighters, gel pens, and stickers.

www.ingramcontent.com/pod-product-compliance
Lightning Source LLC
Chambersburg PA
CBHW020523120726
47904CB00003B/949